THE COUNSELOR

Cormac McCarthy is the author of
eleven acclaimed novels. Among his honours
are the National Book Award, the National
Book Critics Circle Award and the
Pulitzer Prize for Fiction.

THE COUNSELOR

A Screenplay

CORMAC McCARTHY

PICADOR

First published 2013 by Picador

First published in paperback 2013 by Picador
an imprint of Pan Macmillan, a division of Macmillan Publishers Limited
Pan Macmillan, 20 New Wharf Road, London N1 9RR
Basingstoke and Oxford
Associated companies throughout the world
www.panmacmillan.com

ISBN 978-1-4472-2764-9

1 3 5 7 9 8 6 4 2

A CIP catalogue record for this book is available from the British Library.

Printed and bound by CPI Group (UK) Ltd, Croydon, CR0 4YY

THE COUNSELOR

The counselor's condominium bedroom. The curtains are drawn and it is all but dark in the room. The view is from the rear of the bed and of two figures in the bed. The dialogue is muffled at times by the bedcovers and it therefore appears in SUBTITLES on the screen.

LAURA   Are you awake?

COUNSELOR   No.

LAURA   Okay.

COUNSELOR   What time is it?

LAURA   Two oclock. Almost two oclock.

COUNSELOR   Two oclock what.

LAURA   What?

COUNSELOR   AM or PM.

LAURA   You're not serious.

COUNSELOR   Not entirely.

LAURA   It's afternoon.

COUNSELOR   I know. God you're a sexy woman.
            What time is your flight?

LAURA   Seven-forty.

COUNSELOR   What are you doing?

LAURA   I'm not doing anything.

COUNSELOR   They're going to take me out of here on
            a gurney.

LAURA   We could talk.

COUNSELOR   Do you think we should have some
            coffee?

LAURA   You think that we should have coffee.

COUNSELOR   I guess not.

LAURA   I havent seen you for two weeks. And I
            have to go back this evening.

COUNSELOR   I know. Tell me something sexy. Words
            are everything to a man.

LAURA   Okay.

COUNSELOR   Well.

LAURA   I'm thinking.

COUNSELOR   Okay.

LAURA   I want you to put your hand up my dress.

COUNSELOR   You're not wearing a dress.

LAURA   What does that have to do with it? It's something you like for me to say.

COUNSELOR   I know. But it has to be real, doesnt it?

LAURA   All right. I want you to put your hand inside my panties.

COUNSELOR   It's the same problem. Maybe you should just say what it is that you want me to do.

LAURA   I want you to touch me.

COUNSELOR   You want me to touch you where.

LAURA   I want you to touch me down there.

COUNSELOR   You really do.

LAURA	I really do.
COUNSELOR	Say it more sexy.
LAURA	I want you to touch it.
COUNSELOR	God. Are you wet?
LAURA	Yes. Ooh. Baby?
COUNSELOR	God. You're sopping.
LAURA	I know.
COUNSELOR	How did you get yourself into such a state?
LAURA	Ooh. From thinking about you.
COUNSELOR	From thinking about me what.
LAURA	From thinking about your sweet face between my legs.
COUNSELOR	God, woman.
LAURA	Baby? Ooh. I think I should go tidy up.
COUNSELOR	I dont want you to. I want you all over me.

LAURA   Are you sure?

COUNSELOR   Very sure.

LAURA   All right.

COUNSELOR   How did you get to be such a bad girl?

LAURA   It was from hanging out with you. Can I tell you something?

COUNSELOR   Of course.

LAURA   I think you outdid yourself last night. I thought I would never stop coming.

COUNSELOR   You know what that does to a man's ego?

LAURA   I do. Shall I go on?

COUNSELOR   Please.

LAURA   God. Slow. Slow. God. How do you know how to do that?

COUNSELOR   From hanging out with really nasty girls.

LAURA   You've ruined me. You know that.

COUNSELOR   I hope so. God. You have the most lus-
               cious pussy in all of Christendom. Did
               you know that?

LAURA   What do girls say when you do that?

COUNSELOR   There arent any girls. There's just you.

LAURA   But there have been.

COUNSELOR   A long time ago. I dont remember.

LAURA   Yes you do.

COUNSELOR   Do you really want to know?

LAURA   Yes. I do.

COUNSELOR   Okay. They usually would say one of
               two things. Either Oh my God, or
               Jesus Christ. But nearly always some-
               thing religious like that.

LAURA   You're pretty funny.

COUNSELOR   Women like to be amused. Tell me what
               to do.

LAURA   You know what to do.

8

COUNSELOR   Tell me.

LAURA   What if I shock you?

COUNSELOR   Too bad.

LAURA   Are you sure?

COUNSELOR   Yes.

LAURA   Okay. I want you to finger fuck me.

COUNSELOR   What?

LAURA   You heard me.

COUNSELOR   I cant believe you said that.

LAURA   Believe it.

COUNSELOR   You've reached a whole new level of depravity, havent you? I thought that didnt mean that much to girls.

LAURA   Depends on the girl.

COUNSELOR   You really do.

LAURA   I want you to stick your finger up me and find my spot and push on it.

COUNSELOR	Jesus. Right now?
LAURA	No. On Thursday.
COUNSELOR	God.
LAURA	Ooh. God. Yes. Yes. Ooh. I thought you didnt know how to do that?
COUNSELOR	I never said that. God you are luscious.
LAURA	Shh.
COUNSELOR	Okay.
LAURA	Shh. Oh. God. Oh my God.

CREDITS

Mexican garage. A welder in coveralls and goggles is cutting a line along the side of the tank of a Ford F-650 septic-tank truck with an acetylene torch.

Mexican garage. The tank of the truck has been cut in two laterally and a hoist is lowering a fifty-five gallon drum into the open top of the tank. The welder is standing in the tank waiting to unfasten the hooks and the cable.

High desert grassland, similar to the country around Patagonia Arizona or east of Las Vegas New Mexico. Evening.

A white Cadillac Escalade is parked along the edge of an arroyo under some large cottonwood trees. A two-horse trailer is hitched to the rear of the vehicle and the tailgate of the Escalade is down. The driver's door is open and a man— Reiner—is sitting in the driver's seat looking out the open door with a pair of binoculars. He is well dressed in khakis and sport shirt and he is wearing a pair of tall Gokey leather snakeproof boots.

High desert. Evening. A cheetah is loping at high speed.

A street in Amsterdam, shops, canal. The counselor crosses a bridge. He is dressed in a summer suit with no tie and he carries a black nylon portfolio in one hand.

High desert. A very attractive woman—Malkina—is sitting crosslegged in the luggage rack on top of the Escalade. She is wearing a black western hat with a flat or porkpie crown and a braided leather chin strap. A white shirt with a leather vest and a pair of whipcord riding pants with expensive leather boots. Her long black hair is pinned back and she is leaning forward with her elbows on her knees looking through a pair of expensive binoculars.

Mexican garage. The welder is welding the top of the tank back in place.

Mexican garage. The welder is grinding down the weld bead along the side of the tank with an electric disc grinder in a huge shower of sparks.

High desert. A jackrabbit is racing through the grass. The cheetah overtakes it and kills it in a cloud of dust.

High desert. The woman lowers the binoculars and closes her eyes and presses her elbows against her sides. She almost winces. At this close distance we can see the tattoo of an Egyptian cat at the side of her neck. A second cheetah is sitting chained at the side of the Escalade and it gets up and circles and sits again and stares very intently into the distance.

Mexican garage. A man in coveralls wearing a canister paintmask is spraying the tank of the truck in a paintbooth.

Office of a diamond dealer in Amsterdam. An oldfashioned woodpaneled room. The dealer is in shirtsleeves with gaiters, a tie. He pushes the microscope across the table to the counselor. The counselor puts his eye to the microscope. There is a jeweler's blackcloth spread on the desk between them and on it are seven or eight diamonds, three to five carats in size. The counselor looks up and the dealer reaches and pulls the microscope back across the desk and makes a shrugging gesture with one hand and removes the stone from the clip and places it on the blackcloth and mounts another stone in the clip and pushes the microscope back. The counselor bends to study it. The dealer watches him.

A small Mexican port town on the Gulf of California. Several trucks are being unloaded and are driven along the dock toward a warehouse with a sign over the door that says Aduana. *One of the trucks is the septic-tank truck and it is waved aside and the driver hands a brown envelope down to the customs inspector who puts it inside the front of his coat and the truck drives out to the road.*

High desert. Sunset. The woman is riding out across the grasslands at almost a full gallop on a good Arabian horse. English saddle. She turns the horse and looks behind her and bends low over the horse's neck and urges the horse on. The two cheetahs pass her and disappear in the dust.

Southwestern desert. Distant mountains shimmering in the heat. Looking down a long straight stretch of empty blacktop road all but liquid in the waves of heat.

Southwestern desert. The septic-tank truck is sitting in the chaparral. The driver opens the door and stands up, holding onto the roof of the cab and the top of the open door. The other man watches through the windshield with a pair of binoculars. In the distance a line of stragglers crossing through the chaparral, men and women, carrying suitcases, carrying laundrybags over their shoulders. The standing man takes a cigarette from his shirtpocket and lights it and blows the smoke gently.

Office of the diamond dealer.

COUNSELOR   I want her to have something that she would not be uncomfortable wearing. I dont want to give her a diamond so big she'd be afraid to wear it.

DEALER   (*Nodding, just the trace of a smile*) She
              is probably more courageous than you
              imagine.

*He takes the stone from the clip and sorts another one
and puts it in the clip and looks at it through the loupe.
He holds it to his mouth and breathes on it and looks at it
again. He leans and fixes it under the microscope and leans
back. The counselor bends to study the stone. The dealer
watches him.*

COUNSELOR   Is this a Pillow?

DEALER   No. It's an Asscher. Look at the cor-
              ners.

COUNSELOR   Yes.

DEALER   Let's put it in the grading box.

*The counselor looks up and the dealer reaches and takes the
stone with the tweezers from the clip and takes a small white
cardboard trough and places the diamond in it.*

DEALER   The Pillow has a slight arc to the sides.
              It is a modern version of the old-mine
              cut. Let's look at the color.

*The counselor adjusts the microscope and turns the stone with
the tweezers.*

DEALER	Put it table-side down.
COUNSELOR	So you're looking through the pavilion.
DEALER	Yes. There is more to look through.
COUNSELOR	It appears to be yellow.
DEALER	Yes. This is called the body color. It is still a white stone. But the body color will be either brown or yellow. The colors start with D. The D stone has no color.
COUNSELOR	The colors go all the way to Z.
DEALER	Yes.
COUNSELOR	So what am I looking at?
DEALER	H.
COUNSELOR	Is that still a good color?
DEALER	A very good color. It is nitrogen that gives it the yellow. The truth is that anything you can say about a diamond is in the nature of a flaw. The perfect diamond would be composed simply of light. Do you see the inclusion?

COUNSELOR   No.

DEALER   Look some more. It is small. What we
          would call a feather. Turn the stone
          slightly.

COUNSELOR   Yes. I think I see it. *(He looks up and sits
             back)* So it is graded what?

DEALER   A VS-1. Some might grade it higher.

COUNSELOR   You might grade it higher.

The dealer shrugs.

COUNSELOR   You like this stone.

DEALER   I like that stone.

COUNSELOR   How many carats is it?

DEALER   Three point nine.

COUNSELOR   It's expensive.

*The dealer shrugs. He pulls the microscope toward him and
places a stone in the clip and pushes it back.*

DEALER   Tell me what you see. Remember that
          you are not looking for merit. This is a
          cynical business. We seek only imper-

fection. This is a five carat stone. Tell me what you see.

COUNSELOR   *(Bending to the microscope)* This view.

DEALER   Yes.

COUNSELOR   The culet seems big.

The dealer shrugs. The counselor studies the stone.

COUNSELOR   The crown and pavilion dont fit. The girdle comes out crooked.

DEALER   *(Raising his eyebrows)* Yes. The crown and the pavilion may be well cut each in itself and yet stand alien to one another. Once the first facet is cut there can be no going back. What was meant to be a union remains forever untrue and we see a troubling truth in that the forms of our undertakings are complete at their beginnings. For good or for ill.

COUNSELOR   *(Looking up)* But there is no perfect diamond.

DEALER   En este mundo nada es perfecto. As my father would say.

COUNSELOR   You are Sephardic.

DEALER   Yes.

COUNSELOR   Do you know Spain?

DEALER   I do. And Spain me. At one time I
              thought that she would return from
              the grave. But that is not to be. Every
              country that has driven out the jews has
              suffered the same fate.

COUNSELOR   Which is?

DEALER   Ach. You dont want to hear. We should
              talk about the stones. The most val-
              ued stone is the red diamond. From
              the Argyle mines. So very rare. I have
              seen two in a long life. A price almost
              beyond belief.

COUNSELOR   I do want to hear.

DEALER   (Leaning back and studying the counselor)
              You do.

COUNSELOR   Yes.

DEALER   Ach. Well. How to say. There is no cul-
              ture save the Semitic culture. There.
              The last known culture before that was
              the Greek and there will be no culture
              after.

COUNSELOR   That's a bold claim.

DEALER   The heart of any culture is to be found in the nature of the hero. Who is that man who is revered? In the classical world it is the warrior. But in the western world it is the man of God. From Moses to Christ. The prophet. The penitent. Such a figure is unknown to the Greeks. Unheard of. Unimaginable. Because you can only have a man of God, not a man of gods. And this God is the God of the jewish people. There is no other God. We see him—what is the word? Purloined. Purloined in the West. How do you steal a God? The jew beholds his tormentor dressed in the vestments of his own ancient culture. Everything bears a strange familiarity. But the fit is always poor and the hands are always dripping blood. That coat. Didnt that belong to Uncle Chaim? What about the shoes? Enough. I see your look. No more philosophy. And perhaps Schiller is right. When gods were more human men were more divine. The stones themselves have their own view of things. Perhaps they are not so silent as you think. They were piped up out of the earth in a time before any witness was, but here they are. Now, who shall be their witness? We. We two.

Here. *(Fitting a stone in the clip)* This is a cautionary stone.

COUNSELOR   A cautionary diamond.

DEALER   Of course. Why not? Although I suppose every diamond is cautionary. It is not a small thing to wish for, however unattainable. To partake of the stone's endless destiny. Is not that the meaning of adornment? To enhance the beauty of the beloved is to acknowledge both her frailty and the nobility of that frailty. At our noblest we announce to the darkness that we will not be diminished by the brevity of our lives. That we will not thereby be made less. Let me show you. You will see.

Evening. The woman Malkina is sitting in a camp chair at a folding table set with a linen tablecloth, with china and silver. An Aladdin lamp burns on the table and she is reading a book. Reiner places a cocktail glass before her with a cherry in it and leans with a shaker and pours a Manhattan cocktail for her. She looks up and smiles. He goes to the fire and turns two filet steaks on the grill. The two horses are grazing just beyond. The cheetahs at their chains stir, one rises and turns and lies down again. The woman sips her cocktail.

High desert. Evening. Reiner and Malkina are standing on a rise out on the prairie watching the sunset. The sun is about half way down. A vast red sky.

REINER	You like it because it reminds you of Argentina.
MALKINA	It is like Argentina. The Pampas. But that's not why I like it. I like it for itself.
REINER	It doesnt have to be like something else.
MALKINA	No.
REINER	Do I remind you of someone else?
MALKINA	Yes. You do.
REINER	Someone you miss?
MALKINA	Someone who is dead. I dont think I miss things. Things are here and then they are gone. I think to miss them is to hope they will come back. But they are not coming back. I've always known that. Since I was a girl.
REINER	You dont think that's a bit cold?
MALKINA	I think that truth has no temperature. There it goes.

The sun flares out beneath the horizon.

Desert. The sun has just set. Bare purple mountains dark against a darkening sky streaked with deep red. The high thin scream of a motorcycle in the far distance, very slowly becoming louder. Very slowly. Then it streaks across the middle distance in a small part of a second, really just a blink of lights, and whines away into the distance and the silence.

END CREDITS

A small and elegant restaurant in a private club. Some twenty tables, the diners well dressed, the women in cocktail dresses and jewelry. Chandeliers, crystal, silver, linen. Over the sound system Anne-Sophie Mutter is playing Mozart's Violin Concerto No. 2. The waiters are in black tie and black trousers with white kitchen coats. Along one wall are eight large oil portraits of celebrities: Bogart, Monroe, Dean, Elvis, Lennon, Miles Davis, Billie Holiday, and the Spanish Formula One race driver The Marquis de Portago. The paintings are bright and quite striking but neither lurid nor cheap. They are oil paintings that look like really high quality pastels. At the far end of the room there is a raised platform—a small stage—and on the platform is a grand piano. The top of the piano is covered with a red quilt or blanket and it is fastened with bungee cords that go underneath the piano. A cheetah is lying on the piano. The second cheetah comes down through the room past the tables. A woman strokes it absentmindedly as it passes without looking at it. It leaps effortlessly to the top of the piano and sniffs the other cheetah and licks its fur. They wear heavy and elaborate collars with black transponder receivers. On the third wall there is a complete Formula Two Lotus racecar hanging from the actual wall nose down. There is a wall of photographs of cars and drivers and celebrities. At the corner table a man and a woman sit opposite each other. He is forty-three and she is thirty-six. They are well dressed and very attractive. A waiter is clearing the table and another is pouring their champagne flutes. He rewraps the towel around the neck of the bottle and stogs the bottle into the tableside bucket of ice and moves on.

COUNSELOR Anyway, I have something to discuss with you and I'm a bit scared.

LAURA *(Smiling)* Have you been bad?

COUNSELOR No. Actually I dont have that much to discuss. So let me just give you this and you tell me what you think.

He takes a small black velvet box from his coat pocket and places it on the table before her. She puts the back of her hand to her mouth and looks up at him. Then she picks up the box and opens it. She looks up at him again.

LAURA Oh Baby.

COUNSELOR Will you . . .

LAURA Yes. I will.

COUNSELOR Whew.

LAURA   You didnt know?

COUNSELOR   I knew. But I was scared anyway.

LAURA   Good. It's beautiful.

COUNSELOR   Are you okay?

LAURA   Yes. I feel a bit strange.

COUNSELOR   You're not going to cry.

LAURA   No. I dont think so. Are you sure?

COUNSELOR   Oh I'm more than sure.

LAURA   It's beautiful.

COUNSELOR   You are a glory.

LAURA   I'm a glory?

COUNSELOR   Yes. As in glorious. You are a glorious
               woman.

LAURA   Thank you. You are a man of impec-
               cable taste. I shouldnt have said that.

He raises his glass.

COUNSELOR   You cant take it back.

She takes the ring from the box and puts it on her finger and holds out her hand to look at it. She turns her hand to show it to him. She picks up her glass and touches his with it and they drink.

LAURA   Okay then.

COUNSELOR   I intend to love you until I die.

LAURA   Me first.

COUNSELOR   Not on your life.

* * * * *

A small grocery store. A young man dressed in a bright green leather motorcycle outfit—jacket and tight pants and green boots and gloves—is waiting in line, his helmet hanging over his arm. He is somewhat dark. Part Mexican. The woman in front of him has unloaded her groceries onto the conveyor belt and the clerk is adding them up. She turns and smiles at the boy. He is holding a ten-pound bag of dogfood.

WOMAN   Do you have a dog?

YOUNG MAN   Do I have a dog.

WOMAN   *(Smiling)* Yes.

YOUNG MAN   No Mam.

WOMAN   *(A bit disconcerted)* Oh.

YOUNG MAN   I dont have a dog.

WOMAN   Okay.

YOUNG MAN   These are for me.

WOMAN   For you.

YOUNG MAN   Yes Mam. It's a diet.

WOMAN   A diet?

YOUNG MAN   Yes Mam. Well. I probably shouldnt
             even be telling you this. I've tried it a
             couple of times and I got to say it works
             pretty good. You dont really eat. You
             get hungry? You just pop a couple of
             these bad boys. I carry a baggie full
             around with me. Night, you wake up?
             You dont go down and raid the refrig-
             erator. You got a dish of these on the
             table by the bed and you just reach
             and pop a couple. You got your glass
             of water there. Last time I lost twenty-
             seven pounds in thirty days. I'd pretty
             much recommend it to anybody. These
             diets you read about? *(Pointing)* I *know*
             this works. Of course like anything else
             you got to use your head. Time before I

woke up in the hospital. You just got to keep your mind on business. Like anything else. But you want to lose weight? This is it. You got everything you need in here. All your vitamins and minerals. I'll tell you what. After a few days you dont even want anything else. I'd absolutely recommend it to anybody.

The woman turns to the clerk and he gives her back her credit card. The other clerk has finished bagging up her groceries. The boy pushes his bag of dogfood forward.

WOMAN   But you said you woke up in the hospital. What happened? Did you have a systemic reaction or what?

YOUNG MAN   *(Taking out his money to pay for the dogfood)* Oh no Mam. It wasnt anything like that. I was sitting in the street licking my balls and a car hit me. You take care now. You hear?

* * * * *

Reiner's penthouse. A large room giving onto a patio with a swimming pool. There are about twenty people in the room and on the patio—including a number of goodlooking young women. There are tables and chaise longues out at the pool and naked girls splashing in the water. On the outer patio there is a cabana and a bar with a bartender mixing drinks

and a large black weightlifter beside him at an outdoor stain-
less steel grill cooking steaks and ribs. In the room itself are
tables and sofas. There are two waitresses on rollerskates tak-
ing drinks and food to people, one in a bikini and the other in
panties and T-shirt. One of the cheetahs is stretched out on a
sofa and the other is crossing the room. The waitress pulls up
at the bar and orders two Budweisers. Her T-shirt, worn bra-
less, bears a cartoon of a dragster with enormous wheels and
a huge 671 GMC supercharger mounted on the engine. The
script says: Injection Is Nice But I'd Rather Be Blown.
The bartender opens the cooler and takes out two longneck
bottles and calls out Pilsener! and the cook, wearing cut-off
bib overalls, braces himself and the bartender shoves the bottle
into the seat of his overalls and pops the top off the bottle and
then does the same with the second beer and puts them on the
girl's tray and she glides away and pulls up at a coffee table
and sets the beers out and two young women pick them up and
sip from them. On the wall there is an enormous screen which
continually flashes color photos taken of people at parties here.
The counselor passes through the room and comes to a door
where he pushes three buttons on a keypad. He waits. There
is a click and he pushes the door open and enters and turns
and shuts the door. The room is modern and elegant. A bank
of computers and electronic equipment along one wall. An
elegant desk of figured hardwood and stainless steel. Reiner is
sitting on the edge of the desk talking to Malkina, who stands
between his knees. She turns and smiles at the counselor and
Reiner greets him.

REINER   Good morning, Counselor.

COUNSELOR   Morning.

Malkina leans and whispers into Reiner's ear and pats him on the knee and turns to go. She is tall, dark, and very attractive. She smiles again at the counselor as she passes him.

MALKINA   Hola, Guapo.

COUNSELOR   Hey.

She goes out and closes the door and Reiner gets off of the desk and turns his leather swivel-chair and sits in it and motions the counselor to a leather sofa at the end of the desk and at right angles to it. The counselor comes over and sits down.

REINER   How's the bride?

COUNSELOR   Bridal.

REINER   That sounds about right. Nice lady. I assume she's not privy to your newest business venture.

COUNSELOR   She's not. And your lady?

REINER   Yeah.

COUNSELOR   Yeah what.

REINER   She's fine. I dont know what she knows.
                I dont want to know.

COUNSELOR   You dont trust her.

REINER   Jesus, Counselor. She's a woman.

COUNSELOR   Woo.

REINER   Yeah, well. I dont mean it to sound
                that cold. I just mean that where men
                are concerned they've got their own
                agenda. I always liked smart women.
                But it's been an expensive hobby.

COUNSELOR   Yeah. *(Nodding toward the electronic wall)*
                Do you know what all that stuff is?

REINER   Mostly. Anything I dont know I can ask
                her. Which worries me even more.

COUNSELOR   Mmm.

REINER   Yeah.

COUNSELOR   You never told me what happened with
                you and the lovely Clarissa.

REINER   Miss Clarissa. Of the extraordinary
                body. What happened? I think in the
                end it was jealousy that undid us.

COUNSELOR   Jealousy?

REINER   Yeah. She was getting more pussy than I was.

COUNSELOR   *(Smiling)* Is that true?

REINER   I dont know. Probably. I have to say that for a girl who liked girls she took an extraordinary interest in the male member. She sucked on it so hard it finally corrected my vision. She left me for this goodlooking black woman. Had a boyfriend used to play for the Oilers. Nice chap. We met once for drinks at a club in Dallas to discuss our mutual plight. He was taking it rather poorly, I have to say. Women do better, dont they?

COUNSELOR   Maybe they have more practice at it.

REINER   Yeah, well. My guess is that in most cases if you still had the woman you're weeping over you'd be weeping harder.

COUNSELOR   *(Smiling)* You cant hear anything in here, can you?

REINER   It's better than that.

COUNSELOR   Yeah?

REINER   You cant hear anything out there.

COUNSELOR   So is this place secure?

REINER   Who knows? I dont speak in arraignable
              phrases anywhere. There's a scrambler
              on the phone but still there's a lot of
              smart people out there. Of course any-
              body who thinks he's the smartest is on
              his way to the slam.

COUNSELOR   Would that be me?

REINER   Nah. Although I have to say that I
              always did think a law degree was a
              license to steal. And that you for one
              hadnt really capitalized on it.

The counselor shrugs.

REINER   Yeah. Well, you're not the straight dude
              people think though, are you?

COUNSELOR   I guess not.

REINER   I dont mean the caper. I mean you.
              Women like you.

COUNSELOR   All right.

32

REINER   You know what they like about you?

COUNSELOR   I'm a good fuck?

REINER   Yeah, right. They can sniff out the
                moral dilemma. The paradox.

COUNSELOR   Moral dilemma.

REINER   Yeah. They're drawn to it. Not sure
                why. Maybe it's just that lacking any
                moral sense themselves they're fas-
                cinated by it in men. You think about
                it. You want to know if a guy has
                issues watch the way women react to
                him.

COUNSELOR   Interesting.

REINER   Men are attracted to flawed women too
                of course, but their illusion is that they
                can fix them. Women dont want to fix
                anything. They just want to be enter-
                tained. The truth about women is you
                can do anything to them except bore
                them.

COUNSELOR   Well, there's nothing about Laura that
                I would want to fix.

REINER   Maybe not.

COUNSELOR   But you think she probably knows things about me that I dont know about myself.

REINER   Jesus, Counselor. I'm not even sure what sort of a question that is.

COUNSELOR   Yeah. And you? Vis-à-vis your inamorata.

REINER   You dont want to know. I dont want to know.

COUNSELOR   Moral dilemmas.

REINER   Yeah. You pursue this road that you've embarked upon and you will eventually come to moral decisions that will take you completely by surprise. You wont see it coming at all.

COUNSELOR   Such as?

REINER   Such as whether to waste somebody. Or have them wasted.

COUNSELOR   You ever been faced with a decision like that?

REINER   You're a member of the court.

COUNSELOR   Well. I dont intend to take this up as a trade.

REINER   One-time deal. Right?

COUNSELOR   Which you've heard a thousand times.

REINER   No. But a few. What usually happens is that after a couple of deals they know more than you do and they set up shop across the street.

COUNSELOR   How does that work out for them?

REINER   Not well.

COUNSELOR   So would that be a moral issue?

REINER   Not for me.

COUNSELOR   Or for your associates.

REINER   Yeah well. They have a real aversion to mixing business with pleasure. Do you know what a bolito is?

COUNSELOR   No. A bolo is one of those skinny neckties. Or is it one of those things you throw? Argentina.

REINER	Yeah. In this case it's a mechanical device. It has this small electric motor with this rather incredible compound gear that retrieves a steel cable. Battery-driven. The cable is made out of some unholy alloy, almost impossible to cut it, and it's in a loop, and you come up behind the guy and drop it over his head and pull the free end of the cable tight and walk away. No one even sees you. Pulling the cable activates the motor and the noose starts to tighten and it continues to tighten until it goes to zero.
COUNSELOR	It cuts the guy's head off.
REINER	It can.
COUNSELOR	There's nothing he can do.
REINER	No.
COUNSELOR	Jesus.
REINER	Yeah.
COUNSELOR	How long does it take?
REINER	Three, four minutes. Five maybe. It depends on your collar size.

COUNSELOR   You're shitting me.

REINER   Nope. Mostly wretched excess of course.
             It's just that there'd be no easy way to
             turn the thing off. Or reason to. It just
             keeps running until the noose closes
             completely and then it self-destructs.
             Actually you're probably dead in less
             than a minute.

COUNSELOR   From strangulation.

REINER   No. The wire cuts through the carotid
             arteries and sprays blood all over the
             spectators and then everybody goes
             home.

COUNSELOR   Jesus.

REINER   Yeah, well.

COUNSELOR   Bolito.

REINER   Yeah. Probably a play on words too.
             Boleto—with an e—is the spanish
             word for ticket. As in yours has just
             been punched.

COUNSELOR   I wouldnt think it would go through
             bone.

REINER	It wont. It would have to go between the vertebrae. The gear is a worm drive with a gain built into it. Or a reduction, actually. It keeps getting stronger and slower. To compensate for the compression of the tissue.
COUNSELOR	How do you know all this?
REINER	You know how I like gadgets. Anyway, a friend of mine got hold of one. In Calexico. Stolen out of County Property.
COUNSELOR	I would think they'd be expensive.
REINER	They are. This one was used.
COUNSELOR	Sweet.

Reiner shrugs.

COUNSELOR	Why does no one see him?
REINER	See who?
COUNSELOR	The garroteer.
REINER	Oh. Well, given a choice between watching someone walk away down

the street and watching someone being slowly decapitated by a device apparently engineered and patented in the halls of hell you are going to watch the latter. That's just the way it is. You may think you should avert your gaze. But you wont.

COUNSELOR   Where's all this beheading shit come from? You never used to see that.

REINER   Yeah. It's blown in here from the East.

COUNSELOR   Meaning the East.

REINER   Yeah. You put nine Mexicans and an Arab in a room and give them each a hundred dollars and come back in a couple of hours who do you think is going to be holding the grand?

COUNSELOR   So are you gearing up to do business with them down the road?

REINER   The Arabs?

COUNSELOR   Yeah.

REINER   No.

COUNSELOR   Why is that?

REINER   Because they dont need your money.

* * * * *

Southwestern desert. The septic-tank truck and a pickup are parked in the chaparral. The two Mexican drivers are talking to two other men. They squat on the ground. One passes around a pack of cigarettes. Then he picks up a stick and draws a map in the dirt.

* * * * *

A warehouse with floodlights. The metal door clanks upward and the green leather cyclist comes whining through on a Kawasaki ZX-12 and brakes and does a donut on the concrete floor and stops and shuts off the bike and takes off his helmet. A doberman runs to him and stands up and he hugs her and tousles her ears and steps off of the bike. There is a black late-model Cadillac Escalade parked toward the rear of the warehouse. He crosses the room with her leaping about him to an island in the far corner that contains a kitchen and a bed, a tin locker, a leather easy chair—taking the bag of dogfood with him. He fixes her bowl of food and turns on the stereo and opens the refrigerator and takes out a frozen dinner and puts it in the microwave and opens a beer and sits, watching the dog eat. He puts the beer on the table and stands up and takes off the leather jacket and unzips a pocket and takes out a clear plastic bag and pitches it onto the table. It is full of hundred dollar bills. He opens a drawer and takes out a packet of marijuana and papers and sits rolling a joint. He lights it and leans back with his eyes closed. The dog finishes her dish and comes over and circles and sniffs and sneezes. He blows smoke at her and she sneezes and circles.

YOUNG MAN   Yeah, well. Too bad.

The timing bell rings on the microwave. He gets up and goes over and opens the door and takes out the meal. The dog sits watching.

YOUNG MAN   You dont eat lasagna. Go lie down.

*   *   *   *   *

In the club. The counselor and Laura at a table. A young man in a T-shirt, sportcoat, and jeans, with a girl, on their way out. They stop and he pulls back from the girl and smiles at the counselor.

TONY   Well Counselor, how are you making it?

The counselor leans back and studies him.

COUNSELOR   I'm all right.

TONY   Is this your lady?

COUNSELOR   It is.

TONY	How are you, Mam?
LAURA	I'm fine. Thank you.
TONY	Me and the counselor go back a ways. Dont we, Counselor?
COUNSELOR	We do. I'm afraid.
TONY	Dont be afraid, Counselor. Hell, I'm okay with everything. You okay with everything, Counselor?
COUNSELOR	I am if you are.
TONY	*(Addressing Laura)* See there? Aint he just the best son of a bitch?
GIRL	Come on, Tony.
TONY	How long you know this guy, Petunia?
LAURA	Long enough.
TONY	Long enough? How long is that, long enough?
COUNSELOR	Maybe you should listen to your lady friend.
TONY	Is that what you do, Counselor?

COUNSELOR   Pretty much.

TONY   Does he keep you entertained?

LAURA   That's none of your business.

TONY   Because you look to me like you might get bored easy.

GIRL   Tony. Let's go.

TONY   Okay. I'm gone. Here. Let me try this one on you. See if you can tell me what this is. This is pretty good.

He pulls up his T-shirt and places his hands palm down on either side of his navel and moves the skin of his stomach up and down alternately six or eight times very quickly and then spreads them to show his navel. Then he does it again.

TONY   You get it?

Laura has turned away with her eyes closed.

TONY   Let me show you again. Watch.

He repeats the performance.

TONY   Come on, Counselor. It's a girl runnin the hurdles.

Laura bows her head, her eyes closed.

TONY   Come on, Sugardumplin. What? You
              dont think that's funny? She's a little
              up tight aint she Counselor?

The counselor pushes back his chair and stands.

GIRL   Tony I'm going.

TONY   Hell, Counselor. Keep your seat. You
              dont have to get up for me. You know,
              Petunia, the counselor here has got a
              way of sullin up like a possum when he
              dont get his way. I'm goin to say that
              you have probably noticed it. But that
              aint really the problem. The real prob-
              lem is that his thin skin makes it okay
              in his eyes for you to wind up under the
              bus. You know what I'm sayin? Any-
              way, that's how I see it. *(He holds up his
              hands)* All right. I'm goin. I'm goin. You
              take care now. You hear?

                        *   *   *   *   *

*A cafe in a shopping mall. Malkina and Laura are at a table
having lunch.*

MALKINA   So how many carats is it?

LAURA   I dont know.

MALKINA   *(Pausing with a forkful of salad, then putting it down again)* You dont know.

LAURA   *(Smiling)* No.

MALKINA   You have got to be kidding me.

LAURA   No.

MALKINA   Let me see it.

Laura holds out her hand.

MALKINA   No. Take it off.

Laura takes off the ring and hands it across the table to her. Malkina looks at the ring, turns it, holds it up to the light. She hands it back.

MALKINA   It's a three and half carat. Maybe a three point eight. Nice stone. Asscher cut.

LAURA   *(Putting the ring back on)* Thank you.

MALKINA   Good color. Probably an F or a G. Nothing visible so it's at least a VS-2. Do you want to know what it's worth?

LAURA	No.
MALKINA	*(Smiling and shaking her head, stabbing at her salad)* You really dont, do you?
LAURA	No.
MALKINA	So have you set a date?
LAURA	No. I want to get married in the Church. Which he says is all right. He's been married before and I thought that would be a problem but the Church doesnt recognize other marriages. Anyway, I'm looking for a job here.
MALKINA	Are you scared?
LAURA	*(Smiling)* No. A bit nervous. Some-times.
MALKINA	Are you a church lady?
LAURA	I go. Yes. It's important to me.
MALKINA	What about confession?
LAURA	Yes. Well, maybe not so much.
MALKINA	Does the priest ask you about sex?

LAURA	He doesnt ask. But you're supposed to tell him everything.
MALKINA	He doesnt press you for the juicy details?
LAURA	*(Smiling)* No.
MALKINA	He touched me, Father. Where, my child? In the back seat, Father. But you're supposed to go, right?
LAURA	Yes. So you can go to communion.
MALKINA	And whatever nasty shit you did you're supposed to promise not to do it again.
LAURA	Yes.
MALKINA	*(Shaking her head)* Mmm. What if a non-Catholic went in to confess? What would he do?
LAURA	I dont know. Why would you?
MALKINA	I dont know. Maybe because you're only as sick as your secrets. Would he listen?
LAURA	I dont know. He wouldnt be able to give you absolution if you're not a Catholic.

MALKINA   You believe that only Catholics go to
           heaven?

LAURA   I think it's pretty much what the
           Church teaches. I'm not so sure.

MALKINA   Yeah. But anybody could just wander
           into the booth, right?

LAURA   The confessional? Yes. I suppose.

MALKINA   So what do you say?

LAURA   You confess your sins.

MALKINA   Yes, but what do you say? You get in
           there and what? Do you tell him who
           you are?

LAURA   No. You say: Bless me Father for I have
           sinned. And you say how long it's been
           since your last confession. And then
           you tell him what you've done. Then
           when you're through you say that you're
           sorry. Heartily sorry, you say. And that
           you wont do it again.

MALKINA   But you do.

LAURA   I suppose. Usually.

MALKINA	Do you give him any money or anything?
LAURA	No.
MALKINA	*(Shaking her head)* Mmm. Strange. Suppose you've done something really nasty. He doesnt pump you for details?
LAURA	I dont think so. You're embarrassing me.
MALKINA	I can see. You're blushing. Okay. We'll change the subject.
LAURA	Good.
MALKINA	We'll talk about *my* sex life.
LAURA	*(Looking up)* You're teasing.
MALKINA	Just rattling your cage. What a world.
LAURA	You think the world is strange.
MALKINA	I meant yours.

*   *   *   *   *

Northern Mexico at US border. Night. The septic-tank truck is lumbering over the desert, driving with only the parking lights on at the front of the truck. The truck crests a slight rise and grinds to a halt. In the distance are the lights of a city along the horizon.

*   *   *   *   *

A bar at the edge of the city. Afternoon. The counselor comes in and stands at the door for a moment to accustom his eyes to the darkness. Westray is sitting at a table in the corner and he raises one hand. The counselor crosses the room and pulls back a chair and sits at the table. Westray is slightly older than the counselor, nice looking and well dressed. There are very few customers in the bar. At the far end a young man is playing the pinball machine and he gives it a shove and tilts it and walks away. Westray is wearing dark glasses.

WESTRAY   Counselor.

COUNSELOR   It's not dark enough in here for you?

Westray removes the glasses to reveal a black eye.

COUNSELOR   Wow. That's a dandy. What happened?

WESTRAY   Confrontation with a doorman. Who bore a disquieting resemblance to Proconsul.

COUNSELOR   A confrontation?

Westray shrugs.

COUNSELOR   Jesus. What did you say to him?

WESTRAY   I think I told him that he was not to
              take it personally but that he should go
              fuck himself.

COUNSELOR   But not to take it personally.

WESTRAY   No.

COUNSELOR   What did he say?

WESTRAY   He said: I'm going to hurt you, White
              Person. Here she is.

A waitress has arrived at the table. She puts down paper napkins.

WAITRESS   What'll it be?

WESTRAY   I'll have a Heineken.

COUNSELOR   Make it two.

*The waitress glances at Westray's eye and moves away.
Westray sits back in his chair and studies the counselor.*

COUNSELOR   I didnt know that you got into donny-
              brooks.

WESTRAY   I dont. Anyway, that was in another
              country.

COUNSELOR   And besides the wretch is dead?

WESTRAY   No. But I've sent a pair of reliable chaps
             to talk to him. Bloody expensive, too.

COUNSELOR   You surprise me.

WESTRAY   You shouldnt be surprised, Counselor.
             What's the Miller quote that Reiner
             likes? The smallest crumb can devour
             us? You learn to let nothing pass. You
             cant afford to.

COUNSELOR   I should keep that in mind?

WESTRAY   You might keep that in mind. So. Fire
             away.

COUNSELOR   All right. What do you do with the
             money?

WESTRAY   What do I do or what does one do?

COUNSELOR   You.

WESTRAY   Mine goes off shore. We can talk if you
             like. But you cant use my people.

COUNSELOR   All right.

WESTRAY   Let me make a call.

COUNSELOR   All right.

WESTRAY   What else. You're not happy.

COUNSELOR   I'm all right. What's the buy-out for this whole deal?

WESTRAY   Net net?

COUNSELOR   Funny. Yeah. Net net.

WESTRAY   Hard to put a cold dollar on it. You dont know what your expenses are up front. It's six hundred and twenty-five kilos. Pure uncut. It goes for about fifty dollars an ounce in Colombia and the street price in Dallas can be as high as two grand.

COUNSELOR   Is that where it's going? Dallas?

WESTRAY   No. It's going to Chicago. If the whole deal were to go tits up in a ditch the papers would put the street value at a hundred mil. We're probably looking at twenty. Maybe a bit more.

The counselor gets out his pen and starts to write on the napkin.

WESTRAY   It's twenty-one thousand nine hundred ounces.

COUNSELOR   *(Leaning back and studying Westray)* You do that in your head?

WESTRAY   No. I just remembered it. I know somebody who could do it in her head though.

COUNSELOR   Yeah. I'll bet you're right.

WESTRAY   If you're not in, you need to tell me.

COUNSELOR   I'm all right.

WESTRAY   It's not just our people. You've got the money guys. You have to get cash in dollars into Mexico and then they have to get it out again. But that's all they do. You have to use US banks. This means you have to have a corporation. And even then you have to have someone on the inside. You'd be surprised at the people who are in this business. Very surprised.

COUNSELOR   Do you have a corporation?

WESTRAY   No. Of course not. We just pay the points. The other option of course is cash. Which is an even bigger head-ache. For all the obvious reasons. The biggest issue is not that your man is going to fall in love with a poledancer and go south with your ducats. The biggest issue is that somebody is going to figure out who he is and what he's up to. Here we go.

The waitress arrives and sets down the bottles and glasses. The counselor takes a clip of bills from his front pocket but Westray already has a twenty out and he puts it on the tray. She reaches in her apron pocket for change.

WESTRAY   You're good.

WAITRESS   *(Surprised, smiling)* Well thank you.

WESTRAY   I dont suppose you have any pilsener glasses back there.

WAITRESS   Any what?

WESTRAY   It's all right. Thanks.

The waitress moves away.

WESTRAY   I see your look. I like to tip them enough that they dont thank you.

COUNSELOR   Why dont they thank you?

WESTRAY   Because they think it's a mistake. And they dont want to call attention to it.

COUNSELOR   *(Shaking his head and smiling)* Well. Cheers.

WESTRAY   I dont like to be wrong about human nature. Anyway *(Tipping his bottle toward the counselor)* a plague of pustulant boils upon all their scurvid asses.

COUNSELOR   *(Smiling)* Is that your normal toast?

WESTRAY   Increasingly.

COUNSELOR   *(Smiling)* If the drug wars stop this will dry up, right?

WESTRAY   Let's just say it will be more risky. That's the part that Reiner doesnt seem to get. You may have noticed that his lifestyle has become increasingly lavish.

COUNSELOR   I've noticed.

WESTRAY   I never go in his club. And I miss the bastard. We always shared a taste for exotic women. A few times in fact shared the women themselves.

COUNSELOR   That wouldnt include the present one would it?

Westray leans back and studies the counselor.

WESTRAY   And why would you ask me that?

COUNSELOR   No reason. Sorry.

WESTRAY   I see a murky picture forming in your mind. How well do you know her?

COUNSELOR   Not all that well. Why?

WESTRAY   Because you dont know someone until you know what they want. Is why.

COUNSELOR   I'll try and remember that.

WESTRAY   Good.

COUNSELOR   And you're advising me to travel light.

WESTRAY   Yes.

COUNSELOR   And Reiner?

WESTRAY   Reiner thinks that nothing bad can happen. He's in love. Any of this sound familiar? You guys are opening a new club.

COUNSELOR   Is that okay?

WESTRAY   Sure. What the fuck. What else?

COUNSELOR   I dont know.

WESTRAY   Do you know how many people were
               killed in Juarez last year?

COUNSELOR   No. A lot.

WESTRAY   Yes. I think three thousand is a lot. These
               people are another species, Counselor.
               You might want to think about that as
               well. They will rip out your liver and
               eat it in front of your dog.

COUNSELOR   Jesus, Westray.

WESTRAY   Let me ask you this. Before the so-
               called drug wars who do you think was
               killing all those young girls in Juarez?

COUNSELOR   I dont know. Nobody knows.

WESTRAY   Nobody knows.

COUNSELOR   No.

WESTRAY   Come on, Counselor. Hundreds of young
               girls? Thousands, most likely. Follow the
               money. If you have so much cash that

you're using it to insulate your house and you've bought all the cars and clothes and guns that you can find a place to put, and you are morally depraved beyond all human recognition, what then do you spend your money on?

COUNSELOR   Why do they kill them?

WESTRAY   Who knows. For fun. Snuff films. You'll see. Those will start turning up. Anyway, what do you do with a fifteen year old girl that you've just violated with a tiretool?

COUNSELOR   You think the drug lords hire kidnappers to keep them supplied with young girls.

WESTRAY   I think they have kidnappers on full retainer.

COUNSELOR   I guess I should think about that too.

WESTRAY   I cant advise you, Counselor.

COUNSELOR   Yeah. But you are advising me.

WESTRAY   I just want you to be sure that you're locked in. I dont know. Maybe I should tell you what Mickey Rourke told what's-his-face. That that's my recommendation anyway. Dont do it.

COUNSELOR   *(Smiling)* Because I'll tell you something, Counselor. This arson is a serious crime.

WESTRAY   Yes. And so is this.

COUNSELOR   Well. I guess I'm a bit surprised at the cautionary nature of this conversation.

WESTRAY   Good word, cautionary. In Scots Law it defines an instrument in which one person stands as surety for another.

COUNSELOR   As surety.

WESTRAY   Yes.

COUNSELOR   Sounds a bit primitive.

WESTRAY   It is. The problem of course is what happens when the surety turns out to be the more attractive holding.

COUNSELOR   *(Pause)* What about you?

WESTRAY   I can vanish. In a heartbeat. With my money. Can you?

The counselor sits looking out across the room.

WESTRAY   Look, Counselor. The truth is I can walk away from all of this. And I mean all. I know you probably wont believe this but I'll tell you anyway. I think about my life. What have I ever done for the hapless, the hopeless, the horse-fucked? And I'm pretty skeptical about the goodness of the good. I think that if you ransacked the archives of the redeemed you would uncover tales of moral squalor quite beyond the merely appalling. I've pretty much seen it all, Counselor. And it's all shit. I could live in a monastery. Scrub the steps. Wash the pots. Maybe do a little gardening. Why not?

COUNSELOR   You're serious.

WESTRAY   Very.

COUNSELOR   Why dont you?

WESTRAY   In a word? Women.

The counselor smiles.

WESTRAY   I know. But time is not going to stop, Counselor. It's forever. And everything that exists will one day vanish. Forever. And it will take with it every explanation of it that was ever contrived. From Newton and Einstein to Homer and Shakespeare and Michelangelo. Every timeless creation. Your art and your poetry and your science are not even composed of smoke. Alles Vergänglich ist nur ein Gleichnis, as Goethe has it. Everything that perishes is but a likeness. That's really Plato on wheels. A likeness of what? Is that true? I dont want your eyes to glaze completely over, Counselor, but what this is coming down to for me is that seizing the day wont quite do it. I wont flesh out the argument but the only thing ultimately worth your concern is the anguish of your fellow passengers on this hellbound train. I have a lot to answer for. I know that. And I may be a motherfucker but I'm not a hypocrite. You have to help Tom Gray up off the barroom floor. It's little enough. But it's not nothing. All right. Are you ready?

Outside the bar.

WESTRAY   Where are you parked?

COUNSELOR   *(Pointing to his Bentley)* That's me over
              there.

WESTRAY   *(Looking around)* Some neighborhood.
              You're lucky it's still there. Anyway.
              You take care now. You hear?

*The counselor waves and crosses the street. Westray watches
him go.*

WESTRAY   Counselor.

The counselor turns.

WESTRAY   You know why Jesus wasnt born in
              Mexico dont you?

COUNSELOR   No. Why?

WESTRAY   They couldnt find three wise men *or* a
              virgin.

The counselor shakes his head. He turns to go.

WESTRAY   Counselor.

The counselor stops and turns.

WESTRAY   Here's something else for you to con-
              sider. The beheadings and the mutila-

tions? That's just business. You have to keep up appearances. It's not like there's some smoldering rage at the bottom of it. But let's see if we can guess who it is that they *really* want to kill.

COUNSELOR   I dont know. Who?

WESTRAY   You, Counselor. You.

* * * * *

A small and bare conference room for lawyers and their clients at the Texas State Penitentiary for Women. No windows. A table and two chairs. The counselor is standing at the table with his briefcase, going through his documents. The door opens and a guard hands in a woman in prison uniform and closes the door behind her. She is an attractive woman in her early forties.

COUNSELOR   Hey.

RUTH   Did you bring cigarettes?

COUNSELOR   Yeah.

He digs into his briefcase and comes up with a carton of cigarettes and slides them across the table and she sits and starts to open the carton.

COUNSELOR   (*Arranging his files on the table*) I know
             you use those things to trade with but I
             still dont understand what it is that you
             trade for.

RUTH   (*Opening a pack of cigarettes and tapping
             one out*) You dont want to know.

COUNSELOR   They treating you well?

RUTH   Oh yeah. Peachy.

COUNSELOR   You've got a preliminary hearing on
             the seventeenth. What size dress do
             you wear?

RUTH   I wear a seven.

COUNSELOR   What about shoes?

RUTH   Lo mismo.

COUNSELOR   Seven?

RUTH   Yeah.

COUNSELOR   Hat?

RUTH   What?

COUNSELOR   What size hat.

RUTH   Hat? I dont know what size hat. God-
             damn. What do I need a hat for? A hat?
             You're shittin me.

COUNSELOR   Yes.

RUTH   Smart-ass. You had me goin there for
             a minute. *(She lights a cigarette with a
             lighter and looks up and blows smoke.)* You
             goin to get me somethin sexy to wear?

COUNSELOR   No.

RUTH   You'll have me lookin like a fucking
             schoolmarm.

COUNSELOR   How about a business woman?

RUTH   Yeah. Some business.

*She leans back and blows a stream of smoke across the table
and the counselor waves his hand back and forth to waft it
away. He pulls back the chair and sits at the table.*

COUNSELOR   All right.

RUTH   I know you dont think this room is
             bugged but you dont really know that,
             do you?

COUNSELOR   No. Not if you put it that way.

RUTH   I dont know any other way to put it.

COUNSELOR   What was it you wanted to tell me?

RUTH   My kid's in jail.

COUNSELOR   Oh boy. Where?

RUTH   Fort Hancock.

COUNSELOR   Fort Hancock.

RUTH   Yeah.

COUNSELOR   What was he doing in Fort Han-cock?

RUTH   He was comin to see me.

COUNSELOR   What's he in jail for?

RUTH   Speeding.

COUNSELOR   Speeding?

RUTH   Yeah.

COUNSELOR   He couldnt pay the fine?

RUTH   No. He had twelve thousand dol-
            lars on him but they took that off of
            him.

COUNSELOR   Where was he going with twelve thou-
            sand dollars?

RUTH   He was comin here. Like I said.

COUNSELOR   How did you find this out?

RUTH   He called.

COUNSELOR   What else is he charged with?

RUTH   I dont know. Some other stuff. Reck-
            less endangerment or whatever. He said
            they just piled that stuff on on account
            of how fast he was goin.

COUNSELOR   How fast was he going?

RUTH   Two o six.

COUNSELOR   Two o six.

RUTH   Yeah.

COUNSELOR   What is that? Two o six? That's not a
            speed.

RUTH   That's what he said. He didnt want to
                tell me.

COUNSELOR   That's a time of day. Or somebody's
                weight. Two o six? Are you telling me
                he was going two hundred and six miles
                an hour? In what?

RUTH   On that Jap bike of his.

COUNSELOR   Jesus.

RUTH   If you could get him his money back
                he could pay off the fine and get out of
                there.

COUNSELOR   Where did he get the money?

RUTH   I dont know.

COUNSELOR   Well. That's the problem.

RUTH   What's the problem?

COUNSELOR   If you have more than ten thousand
                dollars on you it belongs to the United
                States Government.

RUTH   How is that?

COUNSELOR	Because they say so. If you cant explain where you got it they take it. You might think you should get to keep everything up *to* ten grand and the government would just get the overage but the government doesnt think like that.
RUTH	He aint gettin his money back.
COUNSELOR	No.
RUTH	Well I dont see how you can just take somebody's money.
COUNSELOR	Yeah, well. Welcome to America. How much is the fine?
RUTH	Four hundred dollars.
COUNSELOR	Jesus.
RUTH	I dont guess you'd spring for it, would you?
COUNSELOR	Christ. Four hundred dollars?
RUTH	Yes.
COUNSELOR	All right.
RUTH	All right what?

COUNSELOR	All right I'll get him out.
RUTH	You will?
COUNSELOR	Yeah.
RUTH	Really?
COUNSELOR	Yes really.
RUTH	Thanks. I owe you.
COUNSELOR	Yes you do.
RUTH	How about a blowjob?
COUNSELOR	Well, you'd still owe me three eighty.
RUTH	Damn but you are a smart-ass.
COUNSELOR	I know. You bring it out in me. Lighten up, Ruthie.
RUTH	Dont call me that. I hate that name. I dont even like Ruth.

* * * * *

An inspection station on Interstate 10. Vehicles of various sorts are inching along. The border patrol agent waves several cars past and stops a truck and talks to the driver and then waves him past. The septic-tank truck pulls up and the driver nods and smiles.

DRIVER   How you doin?

AGENT   *(Making an unpleasant face)* All right. Get that thing out of here.

DRIVER   You got it.

The truck pulls away and out onto the highway. The driver shifts gears. He is suddenly a very serious-looking person.

* * * * *

The counselor's condominium. Night. He is sitting in his leather chair with a drink, talking on the phone.

COUNSELOR I know. I just wanted to hear your voice.

Yeah. I really miss you.

Dont go there.

(Chuckling) You're just glowing with sexual health?

No. I love it.

Yes. Bad. Badly.

You havent been taking liberties with your person have you?

(Smiling, almost chuckling) You couldnt touch it with a powder puff?

It's too boring.

I kept waking up thinking you were there. I could smell your perfume on the sheets. I had such an enormous erection I had to get out of bed in order to turn over.

Yes.

In the airport parking lot.

Of course.

Did I know that you would do it with me? Of course.

I dont know. I thought it would be exciting.

Like high school. Yes.

I remember asking you if you were all right. Because you were gasping like an asthmatic.

Of course I remember. What I said was: Here, let me help you off with your damp things. And then I pulled down your panties.

Yes.

Ooh.

Oh my goodness.

Is this phone sex?

I know.

Life is being in bed with you. Everything else is just waiting.

Yes.

I love you very much.

Yes.

You too.

Good night.

He lowers the phone into his lap and leans his head back in the chair with his eyes closed.

Reiner and the counselor in an empty nightclub. Late after-noon.

REINER   You see a place like this in the cold light of day it looks pretty seedy. Everything's lighting, really. Lighting and music. You get the right lighting in here and some music and some goodlooking girls and suddenly it's a whole other world.

COUNSELOR   How soon do you think?

REINER   Two weeks. Three, max.

COUNSELOR   You're keeping the dancefloor.

REINER   Yeah. A dancefloor takes up a lot of space but when you have live music and dancing you have a very different sort of place. The door fees dont really amount to all that much but you can charge more for the drinks. But mostly it's just a different milieu. You try and chat up a girl at a bar? That's a no-man's land. How many guys are good at that? But you ask a chick to dance, well, she doesnt want to look like a bitch. You got a better shot. Sitting at the bar she's supposed to tell you to fuck off. You know Peterson, right?

COUNSELOR   Sure.

REINER   Did you know he speaks portuguese?

COUNSELOR   I didnt know that.

REINER   His mother was from Brazil. She grew up here but her whole family's from Brazil. So this cousin of Peterson's shows up and he speaks about three words of english. If that. This is maybe three years ago. We're all out here on Saturday night and the cousin is asking Peterson how do you say may I have this dance, only we get wind of it and we shut Peterson up and we're coaching the cousin on how you say it. Repeat after me: I. want. to. eat. your. pussy. And we work with him till he's pretty much got it down. I vant to ate you poossy. And we send him off. He's this kind of elegant looking guy anyway. He's wearing a suit and everything. And he goes off across the room and he picks out this really great looking girl and he stands in front of her and gives her this little bow and he says: I vant to ate you poossy. Well. The table gets pretty quiet and this girl looks up at him and she says: What did you say? So of course he says it again. Little bow. I vant to ate you poossy. So she studies him for a minute and then she leans over to see past him and of course here's these three guys across the room all hugging each other and just weeping with merriment and she gets up and she takes Peterson's cousin by the hand and she says something like: Well Buster, this is your lucky night. And she takes him out to this Mercedes van in the parking lot and proceeds to fuck his brains out. He's gone for an hour. We dont know *what* the hell is going on. But everything he's ever heard about American girls is true. Finally she leads him back in and she gives him this big sexy kiss and she cuts her eyes over at us to make sure we're watching and she sends him back to the table. Well. We're going nuts. Peterson is trying to get the story out of him and he's jabbering away and rolling his eyes and we're like, what's he saying? what's he saying? And finally it all comes out. And we're just fucking flabbergasted. No way is this guy lying. We look at the girl across the dance floor and she blows us this big kiss. Jesus. We're just fucking stunned. We want all the details of course and fucking Peterson is feeding it to us in driblets. And of course it's the whole thing. Blowjob. The works. Until we're just sitting there staring at each other. And after a while Peterson gets up and he looks at us and he says: I'm going for it. And off he goes. He crosses the floor to this other table where this really cool looking girl is sitting by herself and he gives her the little bow and announces that he vants to ate her poossy. Well of course about this time the husband is coming out of the mens room and he's about eleven feet tall and he looms up behind Peterson and the girl says: Why dont you tell him what you just told me? Anyway, to make a long story short, this guy hits Peterson so hard that he goes completely across the dancefloor on his back with his arms at his sides and comes up against the wall with his head under a chair and just lies there. Apparently dead. This guy hit him so hard that he came out of his loafers. His loafers are still standing at the table. Peterson is lying dead on the dancefloor in his sockfeet with his head under a chair. Now I know what you're thinking. The guy grabs his wife, throws some money on the table, and they split. Right? Not a bit of it. He sits down and snaps his fingers and they order fresh drinks. Like this is every day for him. Anyway they call an ambulance and they haul Peterson off to the hospital and he's got a concussion and a broken jaw. And his loafers are still at the table.

COUNSELOR   Jesus. What happened with you guys?

REINER   Nothing. We left. We'd had enough fun for one evening. Somebody wanted to go over and get Peterson's loafers but I didnt think that was such a good idea. Anyway. The other big space-eater is the bandstand. They just had a jukebox in here. I think what I'm going to do is take that wall out and get rid of the hallway.

* * * * *

Yard of the Pump Masters Septic Tank Pumping Company. Early morning. The trucks are pulling out one by one and the yard master is checking them off on his clipboard. When they are all gone there is one truck left in the yard.

* * * * *

A large motorcycle store in the city. A man enters and stands looking. He crosses to where a Kawasaki ZX-12 motorcycle is mounted and circling slowly on a motorized dais. The dais is marked off with a blue felt rope and the man approaches and stands looking at the bike for a moment, then unhooks the rope and lets it fall to the floor and mounts the dais and stands circling with it. A clerk talking to a customer nearby sees him.

BIKE CLERK   Excuse me a minute.

The clerk comes over to the dais. The man has taken a steel tape measure from his coat pocket and is measuring the height of the Kawasaki at the handlebars.

BIKE CLERK   Sir, may I help you?

WIRE-MAN   *(Looking at the bike while the steel tape spools up and clicks home. He pops his lips.)* Nope. I'm all done.

The man steps down from the revolving dais and puts the tape measure back in his coat pocket and goes past the clerk toward the door. The clerk bends and picks up the rope and hooks the end of it back in the stand and turns and watches the man as he leaves.

* * * * *

Church, interior. Five women are standing in line along the rear wall of the church waiting to go to confession.

The women are both hispanic and anglo. At the front of the line is Malkina, dressed casually but fashionably. The woman in the confessional pushes back the curtain and exits with her head bowed and Malkina enters the confessional booth.

MALKINA   Hi.

PRIEST   Hi?

MALKINA   Oh. Bless me father for I have sinned.

Silence.

PRIEST   How long has it been since your last confession?

MALKINA   I've never been before. This is my first.

PRIEST   Are you Catholic?

MALKINA   No.

PRIEST   Why are you here?

MALKINA   I wanted to confess my sins.

PRIEST   Have you ever done this before?

MALKINA   No. I told you.

PRIEST   I couldnt give you absolution. Even if
            you did. Confess. You couldnt be for-
            given.

MALKINA   I know. I just wanted to tell someone
            what I'd done and I thought why not go
            to a professional.

PRIEST   Have you thought about taking instruc-
            tions?

MALKINA   That's not something I do very well.

PRIEST   I mean in order to become a Catho-
            lic. You take what are called instruc-
            tions. You learn about the faith. What
            it means. Then you could confess
            and you would be forgiven for your
            sins.

MALKINA   How do you know?

PRIEST   Excuse me?

MALKINA   What if they're unforgivable?

PRIEST   Nothing is unforgivable.

MALKINA   Yeah? What's the worst thing anyone
            ever told you?

PRIEST   I wouldnt be at liberty to tell you a
               thing like that. The priest can never
               reveal anything from the confessional.

MALKINA   That bad, huh? Well, I havent killed
               anybody. But I've been pretty bad. I
               think. I dont really know because I'm
               not all that sure about the rules.

PRIEST   Where are you from?

MALKINA   Buenos Aires. You?

PRIEST   Excuse me?

MALKINA   Where are you from?

PRIEST   Phoenix. Arizona.

MALKINA   I know where Phoenix is. Do you ever
               go out on dates with girls?

PRIEST   No. Of course not.

MALKINA   Boys?

PRIEST   No. What did you want to tell me.

MALKINA   What if I'd done something really bad?
               What if I had killed somebody. Would
               you call the police?

PRIEST   No.

MALKINA   I killed somebody.

PRIEST   You said that you hadnt. Look, I'm
            sorry, but we have people here waiting
            to go to confession.

MALKINA   They can wait. I did. You want to
            throw me out because I'm not a Catho-
            lic but what if I'd said I was one? I
            mean, you dont carry a card around do
            you?

PRIEST   Who did you talk to about this?

MALKINA   Why did I talk to somebody?

PRIEST   You said Bless me father.

MALKINA   I asked a friend. But she didnt know I
            was going to do it. I asked her if non-
            Catholics could go to confession but
            she said no you couldnt.

PRIEST   But you didnt believe her.

MALKINA   No. I believed her. I just wanted to see
            what would happen.

PRIEST   So are we done here then?

MALKINA   I havent told you my sins yet.

PRIEST   I dont want to hear your sins. There would be no point. Are you baptized?

MALKINA   I dont know. It's possible.

PRIEST   Your parents never told you?

MALKINA   I never knew my parents. They were thrown out of a helicopter into the Atlantic Ocean when I was three. Look, you dont have to do the forgiveness thing. All you would have to do is listen. To the sins. You could even pretend I was lying. If you didnt like what you were hearing.

PRIEST   Why would you lie?

MALKINA   I wouldnt. But you could think that I was. Maybe I wanted to be wicked but I didnt have the stones for it. So I would just make up stuff. Women tell you about sex, dont they?

PRIEST   I cant talk about that.

MALKINA   Yes. But every woman who comes to confess tells you that she is an adulterer or a fornicator or something or else why would she be here? The only women who dont come are the ones who arent doing anything. So you must get an unusual picture of women. You must think that they are just having sex all the time. That that's all they do. Anyway, I think that women might make up sexy things to tell you just to make you crazy. Dont you think that's possible?

PRIEST   No.

MALKINA   But you dont know. Suppose I told you that I had sex with my sister. Would you believe that?

PRIEST   You really have to go now.

MALKINA   Because I did. We did it every night. As soon as the lights were out we were at it. We'd be falling asleep at our desks the next day at school. They didnt know what was wrong with us. But that's not the worst thing. Where are you going?

The priest pushes back the curtain and exits the confessional. Malkina, kneeling, turns and pushes aside the curtain. The priest is hurrying up the aisle, blessing himself.

MALKINA   *(Standing up and calling to the priest)* Wait! I wasnt finished!

The women waiting to go to the confession are confused, horrified. One of them blesses herself.

* * * * *

Border city. Evening. An outdoor cafe adjoining a parking lot. Metal chairs and tables. Traffic. A Mexican man is sitting at one of the tables with a cup of coffee before him and a newspaper. The young man in green pulls up on the Kawasaki ZX-12. He takes off the gloves and the helmet and puts the gloves inside the helmet and steps off of the bike and walks down to where the man is sitting and kicks back a chair and sits down.

A man and a girl are sitting in a parked car. The girl is watching the table through a pair of binoculars.

GIRL   I wont be able to get what the kid is saying. Is that okay?

MAN (JAIME)   We dont care what the kid is saying.

She is watching through the binoculars and writing on a pad on a clipboard.

The man at the table rises and leaves, leaving the paper on the table. The kid sits at the table and opens the newspaper and sits reading.

JAIME   Did you get it?

87

GIRL   Yeah. It's not much.

JAIME   That's okay. Keep your eye on him.

GIRL   I am.

JAIME   This guy doesnt read the fucking news-
              papers.

GIRL   I know.

*The kid rakes an object from under the paper into his hel-
met and puts down the paper and stands and puts the helmet
under his arm and crosses the plaza to his bike and puts his
foot over the bike and starts it with the starter and pulls his
gloves from the helmet and lays them on the tank in front of
him and pulls on the helmet and fastens the strap and then
pulls on the gloves and kicks back the stand and pulls away
into the traffic.*

JAIME   Could you see what it was?

GIRL   No. But it's in the helmet.

JAIME   Yeah. It's in the helmet.

The man is dialing a number on his cell phone.

* * * * *

Reiner's house. Malkina is on the phone.

MALKINA   Look Jaime, he doesnt have to know,
                 he just has to do what I tell him to
                 do. No. It's already downloaded. It's
                 programmed to pick up the bike at
                 above five thousand rpm's and that
                 is coded into the global. The only
                 way we can lose him is if he suddenly
                 decides not to drive over thirty miles
                 an hour and I'll leave you to think
                 about how likely that is. Call me in an
                 hour.

*Jaime and the girl in the parked car. Jaime clicks off the cell
phone and looks at the girl.*

JAIME   Let's go.

                     *   *   *   *   *

Corner table in an upscale club. The counselor and Reiner.

REINER   I dont know. Women have funny ideas
                 about sex. They're supposed to be so
                 modest? Let me tell you. When they get
                 it into their head that they want to fuck
                 they're like a freight train. The things
                 I've learned about women? Fuck. About
                 half of it I'd like to forget.

He takes a sip of his drink.

COUNSELOR   I'm not sure I follow you. What is it you'd like to forget? For instance.

REINER   You dont want to know.

COUNSELOR   Sure I do.

REINER   Not the worst things.

COUNSELOR   Those in particular.

REINER   Not the very worst.

COUNSELOR   Come off it, Reiner.

REINER   I dont know. Let's talk about something else.

COUNSELOR   Are you shitting me? What else?

REINER   Yeah. I dont know. I shouldnt tell you this.

COUNSELOR   Just pull up your socks and tell me. What is it you'd like to forget?

REINER   All right. I'd like to forget about Malkina fucking my car.

COUNSELOR   What?

REINER   See?

COUNSELOR   What did you just say?

REINER   I said I'd like to forget about Malkina
            fucking my car. I think.

COUNSELOR   What the hell are you talking about?

REINER   You remember the 328 I had.

COUNSELOR   Sure. Nice car.

REINER   Very nice car. Not a V-12 but a better
            car than the 308. Which was an embar-
            rassment for a Ferrari. Westray had one
            and he said that it wouldnt pull a greasy
            string out of a cat's ass. His metaphor.
            Is that a metaphor? Anyway, this was a
            while back. Not that long. We'd been
            getting it on for a while and we came
            back one night—we were staying up
            at Cloudcroft. Mostly for that great
            stretch of road between Cloudcroft
            and Ruidoso. And we drove out on the
            golf course and parked and we're sit-
            ting there talking and for no particular
            reason that I could see she lifts herself
            up and slides off her knickers and hands
            them to me and gets out of the car. I

asked her what she was doing and she says: I'm going to fuck your car. Jesus. She tells me to leave the door open. Turns out she wants the domelight on. So she goes around and climbs up on the hood of the Ferrari and pulls her dress up around her waist and spreads herself across the windshield in front of me with no panties on. And she's had this Brazilian wax job. And she begins to rub herself on the glass. Dont even think I'm making this up. You cant make this up. I mean, she was a dancer, right? In Argentina? She danced at the opera thing down there. I've seen the clippings. And she does this full split and starts rubbing herself up and down on the glass and she's lying on the roof of the car and she leans down over the side to see if I'm watching. Like, no, I'm sitting there reading my e-mail. And she gestures at me to crank down the window and she leans in and kisses me. Upside down. And then she tells me that she's going to come. And I thought, well, I'm losing my fucking mind. That's what's happening here. It was like one of those catfish things. One of those bottom feeders you see going up the side of the aquarium. Sucking its way up the glass? It was just. I dont know. It was just . . . Hallucinatory. You see a thing like that, it changes you.

COUNSELOR   Jesus.

REINER   Tell me about it.

COUNSELOR   Did she?

REINER   Did she what?

COUNSELOR   Did she come?

REINER   Yeah. Sure. Then she just laid there. Spread out across the windshield. Finally she climbs down and comes around and gets in the car and shuts the door and I hand her her knickers and she puts them in her purse and she sort of looks at me. Like to see what I thought about that. What I thought about that? Jesus. I dont know what I thought about that. I still dont. It was too gynecological to be sexy. Almost. But mostly I was just fucking stunned. Maybe I was thinking about the leather. I dont know.

COUNSELOR   The leather.

REINER   Yeah. The seats. You know. Where she was sitting? I mean the car is about two weeks old. Finally I asked her if she'd ever done that before and she said she'd done everything before. Of course. So I start the engine and turn on the lights but the windshield is all smeared and I didnt have anything to wipe it with and of course she suggested that I get out and lick it off and I tried the wipers but naturally the windshield washer thing doesnt work because the Italians dont really believe in that sort of thing and finally I took off my socks and got out of the car and used them.

COUNSELOR   Catfish?

REINER   I dont know. Yeah. I think so.

COUNSELOR   Do you think she knew the kind of effect this might have on a guy?

REINER   Jesus, Counselor. Are you kidding? She knows everything.

COUNSELOR   You dont think this is an odd thing to tell me?

REINER   I think it's an odd thing.

COUNSELOR   Yes, but I mean why would you tell me
             this? I mean, I know this woman. Why
             is it okay to tell a thing like that about
             somebody . . .

REINER   Somebody I'm banging?

COUNSELOR   Come on, Reiner.

REINER   I dont know. You're probably right. May-
             be I wanted to see what you'd say. Maybe
             there's more to it than that. Maybe I'm
             scared.

COUNSELOR   You're scared?

REINER   Yeah. Probably. Yeah. Sometimes she
             scares the shit out of me.

COUNSELOR   Because of that?

REINER   No. Not that.

COUNSELOR   You're in love with her.

REINER   I dont know what I am. Yeah. I suppose
             I am in love with her. You dont think
             that's cause for worry? It's like being in
             love with . . . what? Easeful death? Fuck
             it. Fuck it, Counselor. Just forget the
             whole thing.

95

COUNSELOR   It's just that I dont know what it is that you're trying to tell me.

REINER   I know.

COUNSELOR   Does this have anything to do with the deal?

REINER   I dont know. You're right. I shouldnt have told you. Just forget it.

COUNSELOR   Forget it.

REINER   Yeah.

COUNSELOR   How do you propose that I do that?

REINER   I dont know. Jesus, Counselor. How do I know?

*   *   *   *   *

Malkina's bedroom. She sits in a robe in front of the fire. The cheetahs are lying on the rug at her feet. She is listening on the phone.

LAURA   No. I had a dream about you. And when I woke up I couldnt remember why the dream was so troubling even though I could still remember the dream. I just wanted to call and see if you were all right.

MALKINA   Are you superstitious?

LAURA   I dont think so. No more than the next person.

MALKINA   And who would that be?

LAURA   Excuse me?

MALKINA   The next person. You're not gay are you?

LAURA   No. Of course not. I shouldnt have called. I know you think my world naive. But is that so bad?

MALKINA   I dont know. I cant advise you.

LAURA   I know.

MALKINA   You should be careful what you wish for, Angel. You might not get it.

LAURA   I know.

MALKINA   Do you?

LAURA	Yes. I do.
MALKINA	Good. I'll see you at the club.

* * * * *

Two-lane blacktop road through the high desert. Night. A car passes and the lights recede down the long straight and fade out. A man walks out from the scrub cedars that line the road and stands in the middle of the road and lights a cigarette. He is carrying a roll of thin monel wire over one shoulder. He continues across the road to the fence. A tall metal pipe is mounted to one of the fenceposts and at the top—some twenty feet off the ground—is a floodlight. The man pushes the button on a small plastic sending unit and the light comes on, flooding the road and the man's face. He turns it off and walks down the fence line a good hundred yards to the corner of the fence and here he drops the coil of wire to the ground and takes a flashlight from his back pocket and puts it in his teeth and takes a pair of leather gloves from his belt and puts them on. Then he loops the wire around the corner post and pulls the end of the wire through the loop and wraps it about six times around the wire itself and tucks the end several times inside the loop and then takes the wire in both hands and hauls it as tight as he can get it. Then he takes the coil of wire and walks out and crosses the road, letting out the wire behind him. In the cedars on the far side a flatbed truck is parked with the bed of the truck facing the road. He walks up to the rear of the truck and turns and pulls the wire taut and shines his flashlight back along the length of it. There is an iron pipe at the right rear of the truckbed mounted vertically in a pair of collars so that it can slide up and down and the man threads the wire through a hole in the pipe and pulls it taut and stops it from sliding back by clamping the wire with a pair of visegrips. Then he walks back out to the road and takes a tape measure from his belt and measures the height of the wire from the road surface. He goes back to the truck and lowers the iron pipe in its collars and clamps it in place again with a threaded lever that he turns by hand against the vertical rod. He goes out to the road and measures the wire again and comes back and wraps the end of the wire through a heavy three-inch iron ring and walks to the front of the truck where he pulls the wire taut and wraps it around itself to secure the ring at the end of the wire and then pulls the ring over a hook mounted in the side rail of the truck bed. He stands looking at it. He strums the wire with his fingers. It gives off a deep resonant note. He unhooks the ring and walks the wire to the rear of the truck until it lies slack on the ground and in the road. He lays the ring on the truck bed and goes around and he takes a walkie-talkie from a work-bag in the cab of the truck and stands in the open door of the truck listening. He checks his watch by the domelight in the cab.

WIRE-MAN   Anything?

VOICE (MALE)   He's coming.

WIRE-MAN   You're at eight miles.

VOICE   Yeah.

WIRE-MAN   That's less than three minutes.

VOICE	Yeah. Flat out it's about two minutes and twenty seconds.
WIRE-MAN	Can you hear him?
VOICE	Not yet.

They wait.

VOICE	There he is.
WIRE-MAN	Yeah. I hear him. All right. Let's do it.

He hangs up the walkie-talkie and takes the cigarette from his mouth and grinds it into the dirt and shuts the door of the truck. He looks at his watch. Very thin in the distance we can hear the highpitched scream of the Kawasaki bike flat out at eleven thousand rpm.

Shot of the green rider bent low over the bike at one hundred and ninety miles an hour. Suddenly the floodlight comes on and he raises up and turns his head to look at it.

The truck. The desert is suddenly lit to the north of the wire-man and he takes the ring and carries it forward and pulls it over the hook. The wire hums.

Shot of green rider with his face turned back to the floodlight now behind him. Suddenly his head zips away and in the helmet it goes bouncing down the highway behind the bike. The bike continues on, the motor slows and dies to silence, and in the distance we see a long slither of sparks recede into the dark.

The truck. The man clips the wire at the ring with a pair of wirecutters and the wire zips away. He walks out to the road with the walkie-talkie. In the road he shines the light down the blacktop and then walks down the roadside ditch until he comes to the helmet.

WIRE-MAN   *(Into walkie-talkie)* We're good. Yeah. Over and out.

He puts away the walkie-talkie and bends over and picks up the helmet. It is surprisingly heavy. He goes back to the truck and opens the cab door on the driver's side and puts the helmet in the floor and shuts the door and goes out to the road and crosses to the fence where he cuts the wire free from the fence-post and begins to wind it up as he walks, passing the wire over his elbow at each turn to make a coil of the wire. At the truck he stows the wire in a toolbox under the bed of the truck and gets in the truck and starts it and turns on the lights and turns out into the road.

Desert. Night. At the fence the man is disassembling the pole and floodlight. Disconnecting the wires. The pole is made of sections of 1-5/8 inch galvanized chainlink fencepost that slide one into the next and he puts these in the bed of the truck and puts the small components in the under-bed toolbox.

Desert. Night. The truck pulls out and drives past the head-less body sprawled in the road. Then it stops. The man looks out the window of the truck back at the body, then backs up the truck and gets out. He picks up the feet and drags the body into the ditch and wipes his hands on his pants and then gets back in the truck and pulls away down the highway.

* * * * *

Death row cell, Texas State Penitentiary. Night. Ruth wakes and lies looking up at the ceiling. She sits up, pushing back the bed covers. She sits on the edge of the bunk with her hands folded.

* * * * *

Front gate of the septic-tank company. The flatbed truck pulls up and the wire-man gets out and shuts the door. He is holding a battery-driven diegrinder in one hand and he watches the road behind him where a single light is approaching. Sound of a motorcycle. The cycle pulls up and halts and the rider gets off and kicks down the stand and the wire-man goes to the gate and turns on the diegrinder and bends to cut the padlock on the gate. A sheaf of sparks lights up the area and the lock falls to the ground in about twenty seconds. He pushes open the gate and then bends and picks up the lock and juggles it in his hand and throws it into the bushes.

WIRE-MAN   *(Shaking his hand)* Hot son of a bitch.

The second man goes past and turns on a flashlight.

SECOND MAN   You know which one it is?

WIRE-MAN   Yeah. It's got Arizona plates.

The wire-man goes back to the flatbed truck and opens the passenger side door and takes the green motorcycle helmet off the seat and takes out of the helmet a set of keys and a computerized jumper cable with three color coded jacks and shuts the door and follows the second man into the yard where the septic-tank trucks are parked. The second man has opened the door of the truck and pulled the hood release and he goes around to the front of the truck and opens the hood.

WIRE-MAN   Let me see your light.

He takes the light and goes along the side of the truck and picks up a loose set of wires.

SECOND MAN   You know how it goes?

WIRE-MAN   Yeah. It's color coded. Red to red, green to green. Black to black. Here. Hold the light.

He plugs in the connections and hands the keys to the second man.

WIRE-MAN   See if it'll start.

The second man gets in the truck and turns the key. He turns it again.

WIRE-MAN   Wait a minute. This thing's got a switch
             on it. How do you say *on* in Mexican?

SECOND MAN   You're shittin me.

WIRE-MAN   Try it now.

The second man cranks the engine and it starts. Wire-man drops the hood and steps back.

* * * * *

The counselor is sitting in his chair in his condo, listening to Westray on the telephone.

WESTRAY   Counselor.

COUNSELOR   Que pasó?

WESTRAY   We've got a problem.

Silence.

WESTRAY   You there?

COUNSELOR   I'm here. How bad a problem?

WESTRAY   Let's say pretty bad. Then multiply by
            ten.

COUNSELOR   Fuck.

WESTRAY   What time can you meet me tomor-
            row?

COUNSELOR   It is tomorrow.

WESTRAY   What time?

COUNSELOR   Nine oclock.

WESTRAY   All right. Where.

COUNSELOR   How about the coffeeshop at the Coro-
            nado.

WESTRAY   How about McDonald's? We can start
            getting used to our new lifestyle.

COUNSELOR   *(Softly)* Jesus. Coronado. Nine oclock.

WESTRAY   See you at nine.

*The counselor hangs up the phone and leans back and puts his
hand over his eyes.*

COUNSELOR   Fuck. Fuckety fuck fuck fuck fuck.

* * * * *

Coffeeshop of an elegant downtown hotel. The counselor is seated at a corner table watching Westray enter and scan the room. Westray is dressed in a goodlooking suit, no tie. Carrying a newspaper. The counselor looks at his watch. Westray crosses the room to the table.

WESTRAY   Morning.

COUNSELOR   Good morning.

Westray lays the paper on the table and sits.

WESTRAY   You seen the paper?

COUNSELOR   No.

The waitress puts down menus and glasses of water. She knows the counselor and flirts a bit with him. They wait till she has gone before they talk again.

WESTRAY   Do you know who the Green Hornet is?

COUNSELOR   The Green Hornet.

WESTRAY   Yes.

COUNSELOR   He's a cartoon character.

WESTRAY   It's all right. The newspaper doesnt
                 know either. He's a biker.

COUNSELOR   Shit. *(Leaning back)* All right. What? Is
                 he in custody?

WESTRAY   In a manner of speaking, yes.

The counselor reaches for the paper.

COUNSELOR   It's in the paper? What has he done?

WESTRAY   You dont know anything about this.

COUNSELOR   *(Thumbing through the paper)* About what?

The counselor stops and looks at Westray.

COUNSELOR   What?

Westray holds out his hand in a gesture that says: Go ahead.

WESTRAY   Like I said: They dont even know who
                 he is.

COUNSELOR   He had no ID on him.

WESTRAY   No. No ID. And no head, actually.

COUNSELOR   No head?

WESTRAY   Mmm.

The counselor sits reading. He looks up.

COUNSELOR   What the hell is this? Does his mother
               know?

WESTRAY   Oh yes. She thinks they'll probably get
               to her before the State does. Anyway
               they did find his head. Read on. Read
               the part where it says it appeared to
               have been thrown from the window of
               a car at speed. I sort of liked that. Car
               at speed.

COUNSELOR   *(Reading)* Mother of God. *(Looking up)*
               A police spokesperson said the matter is
               under further investigation?

WESTRAY   I hope you havent done something stu-
               pid.

COUNSELOR   *(Pushing the paper aside)* All right. Why
               dont you tell me what this is about.

WESTRAY   I thought you might be able to tell me.
               I had a call from our business partners.
               They wanted to talk with you.

COUNSELOR   Do I want to talk to them?

WESTRAY   I dont think so. In these circles talk has
               a slightly different meaning. Anyway,
               it seems that the deceased was working
               for them. Now the shipment is missing
               and the only thing they have to go on is
               that he was a client of yours.

COUNSELOR   Client? He wasnt a client. I paid a
               speeding ticket for him.

WESTRAY   Well. I'm perfectly willing to believe
               you had nothing to do with this but I'm
               not the party you have to convince.

COUNSELOR   Convince of what, for Christ sake?

WESTRAY   That this is just some sort of coinci-
               dence. Because they dont really believe
               in coincidences. They've heard of them.
               They've just never seen one.

COUNSELOR   God. So what happened to the ship-
               ment?

WESTRAY   I asked them that.

COUNSELOR   And?

WESTRAY   They said: Se fue.

COUNSELOR   Se fue? Jesus.

WESTRAY   Mmm.

COUNSELOR   I need to call his mother.

WESTRAY   Probably not such a good idea.

COUNSELOR   Why is that?

WESTRAY   She says she's going to have you killed.

COUNSELOR   Sweet Jesus.

The waitress comes to the table.

WAITRESS   Sorry about that. What can I get you to
               drink?

COUNSELOR   Hemlock.

WAITRESS   I'm sorry?

WESTRAY   I'd like an orange juice and coffee and
               he's having a double Maalox with a side
               of Oxycontin.

*The waitress looks from one to the other, tapping her pencil
on her order pad.*

WESTRAY   Sorry. Just bring us two coffees. And
               my OJ.

The waitress moves away.

WESTRAY   How did you wind up with her?

COUNSELOR   The mother?

WESTRAY   The mother. The mother of all moth-
            ers.

COUNSELOR   It was a court appointment. An appeal.
            One of Ferguson's fucked up deals.
            Look. They cant hook me up to this.
            What do they think I would *do* with the
            stuff?

WESTRAY   They dont know. They dont care. They
            assume that everybody knows some-
            body. They do. You need to think about
            this, Counselor. These people are out
            twenty mil. Do you know how serious
            that is?

The counselor sits back and studies Westray.

COUNSELOR   They think we're all involved.

WESTRAY   Why wouldnt they?

COUNSELOR   Reiner too.

WESTRAY   Yes. You fucking genius.

COUNSELOR *(Looking away)* Jesus.

The waitress returns and sets down their coffee and the juice.

WAITRESS Did you want to order?

WESTRAY No thanks. We've sort of lost our appetites.

COUNSELOR This is fine, Alexis.

The waitress moves away.

WESTRAY Have you ever seen a snuff film?

COUNSELOR No. Have you?

WESTRAY No. Would you?

COUNSELOR I would not.

WESTRAY Because the consumer of the product is essential to its production. You cant watch without being implicated in a murder.

COUNSELOR But you know someone who's seen one.

WESTRAY I do. He said that the girl was beheaded with a machete. She was about fourteen and she was being sodomized by a hooded figure and looking into the camera and crying when her head fell off.

COUNSELOR   Jesus.

WESTRAY   You might want to think about that the next time you do a line.

COUNSELOR   I dont do drugs.

WESTRAY   I'm glad to hear that, Counselor. Because it's what was done to her next that you really wouldnt want to see. I wont ask you to use your imagination because I sincerely hope that it wouldnt be up to the task. They led forth a portly and slightly older fellow naked and erect and wearing like the others a black hood with eyeholes. To address himself to the naked and quivering and headless corpse in all its gushing menses which you must remember would not have served his purpose had she not been young and pretty. And all of this he has paid for. Now. What do you think it cost? Ballpark.

The counselor sits with a blank face. Then suddenly he grimaces and turns his face away.

COUNSELOR   Oh Jesus.

WESTRAY   Mmm.

COUNSELOR   God. Do you think that's true?

WESTRAY   I know it's true.

COUNSELOR   There cant be such people.

WESTRAY   Think again, Counselor.

COUNSELOR   Good God.

WESTRAY   The point, Counselor, is that you may think that there are things that these people are incapable of. There aren't.

The counselor sits staring at the table. Westray sips his coffee. The counselor raises his head and looks at him.

WESTRAY   It's always later than you think, Counselor. I should have jumped ship a long time ago and I didn't.

COUNSELOR   What are you going to do?

WESTRAY   Me? I'll be gone in no time at all.

COUNSELOR   Where will you go?

WESTRAY   Yeah, right.

COUNSELOR   You think I'd rat you out.

WESTRAY   Counselor, if these people got hold of
            her the Virgin Mary would rat you
            out.

COUNSELOR   Jesus.

WESTRAY   I've known this was coming for a long
            time. For all my sins I still believe in a
            moral order. I'm not so sure about you.
            And it's not that you're going down,
            Counselor. It's what you're taking down
            with you. All right. Take care.

He rises and leaves.

* * * * *

An upscale restaurant.

MALKINA   So where do you think this is going, mi
            Capitan.

REINER   This?

MALKINA   Yes.

REINER   I cant really take your question seri-
              ously. It's going where it's going.

MALKINA   Either you think everything is going
              to be okay or you dont want to think
              about it at all.

REINER   Because the third possibility is not
              something you're ready to admit to.

MALKINA   Yes. The excluded middle. The Ter-
              tium non Datur.

REINER   I dont know, Baby Girl. You read that
              stuff, I dont. *(Pause)* I dont like deci-
              sions made for me. But if you put them
              off, waiting for the maximum informa-
              tion, that might be what happens. You
              think that there is still space enough to
              make the decision. And then there isnt.

MALKINA   Space.

REINER   Yes.

MALKINA   Greed always takes you to the edge,
              doesnt it?

REINER   That's not what greed does. That's
              what greed is.

MALKINA   You know that when the axe comes
             through the door I'll already be gone.
             Dont you.

REINER   That's fair enough.

MALKINA   I'm not entirely faithless. You'll see.

Reiner smiles.

MALKINA   You're in trouble.

REINER   Probably.

MALKINA   What do you want me to tell you?

REINER   I dont know. What do you?

MALKINA   I dont know. I miss the ladies.

Reiner tilts his head. Almost a shrug.

MALKINA   I dont know what I can tell you.

REINER   About the ladies?

MALKINA   No. Not about that.

REINER   You'll figure it out.

MALKINA	I know. But the space is closing fast. I know that. The space that you spoke of.
REINER	I dont want to lose you. There.
MALKINA	I know.
REINER	Are you hungry?
MALKINA	I'm starving.

* * * * *

Reiner's office. The counselor is pacing up and back. He stops and turns.

COUNSELOR	You talked to him.
REINER	Yeah. I talked to him.
COUNSELOR	Can we go somewhere?
REINER	*(Rising)* Sure.
COUNSELOR	I dont feel comfortable in here.
REINER	Come on.

* * * * *

Booth in a coffeeshop.

REINER   You asked me that.

COUNSELOR   Yeah. But you didnt answer that.

REINER   You think I know something you dont.
                Maybe I think the same thing.

COUNSELOR   I've told you everything I know.

REINER   What are you going to do?

COUNSELOR   I dont know. What are you?

REINER   I dont know.

COUNSELOR   That's what Westray said. But he did
                know. Didnt he?

REINER   I know you dont have any money or you
                wouldnt be in this jackpot in the first
                place.

COUNSELOR   Maybe.

REINER   Yeah. Well. I know why I'm in it. Do
                you?

COUNSELOR   Sure. Same as you. Greed.

REINER   I dont think so. You got in trouble. I
              tried to appeal to your greed two years
              ago. No deal. Now it's too late. Greed
              is greatly overrated. But fear isnt.

COUNSELOR   What do you think I should do?

REINER   I dont know, Counselor. They know
              that you're stupid. They just dont know
              how stupid.

COUNSELOR   You say that like it's my hole card.

REINER   Maybe it is.

COUNSELOR   Maybe I could talk to them.

REINER   And say what?

COUNSELOR   I'd tell them the truth.

REINER   You're just a fucking wonder. Did you
              know that? Go ahead.

COUNSELOR   Go ahead what?

REINER   With the truth. I'd like to hear it.

COUNSELOR   I'd tell them that I'd never even met this
              kid. That I'd gotten him out of jail on a
              speeding charge.

REINER   Okay. How did he happen to hire you?

COUNSELOR   He didnt. I got him out of jail as a favor
              to his mother.

REINER   Okay. How did you happen to know the
              mother?

COUNSELOR   I was appointed by the court to repre-
              sent her in an appeal on a capital mur-
              der case. She killed her husband. The
              kid's stepfather.

REINER   Did you know what the kid did for a
              living?

COUNSELOR   No.

REINER   But you do now.

COUNSELOR   I do now. Yes.

REINER   And would it please you to tell the court
              what that occupation was?

COUNSELOR   How did I get in court?

REINER   Sorry. I guess I was getting ahead of
              myself.

COUNSELOR   Very funny.

Reiner stirs his coffee. He lays the spoon steaming on the table.

REINER   Yeah. Well. Probably not.

* * * * *

The counselor is on a busy street downtown. It is raining. He turns into a cafe and approaches a woman sitting at a table with a poodle.

COUNSELOR   Mam, I'm terribly sorry to bother you but my phone is out and it's something of an emergency. Could I use your phone for just a minute?

The woman looks at him and then hands him her phone which is lying on the table. The counselor dials.

COUNSELOR   Where are you?

I cant call you on my phone.

No. You cant.

Go to a hotel and call me later.

Dont go to the apartment.

Just dont.

It's very important.

I've got to go.

Dont call anyone.

No.

Anyone. I love you.

He rings off and hands the woman her phone.

COUNSELOR   Thank you very much. Very kind of you.

He turns and goes out. The woman finishes her coffee and rises with the dog under her arm and goes out. She puts up her red umbrella and stands holding the poodle and looking out at the street in the rain.

* * * * *

The septic-tank truck on a two-lane blacktop road in central Texas. A late-model sedan is following it, two men in the car. The passenger in the sedan plugs a flashing red rooflight into the cigar lighter in the dash and reaches out the window and places the light on the roof of the car. Then he takes a black box off the seat and holds it at the window and turns it on and it begins to emit a police siren sound. The septic-tank truck slows and pulls over onto the verge and comes to a halt. The sedan pulls in some distance behind it and the two men get out, putting on white Stetson hats. They are dressed in boots and tan slacks and white shirts and wear automatic sidearms.

The driver of the truck—wire-man—watches them in the rearview mirror. The boots of the co-driver of the truck are moving back along the passenger side of the truck. The driver starts the truck and pulls away. The two men in the road have almost reached the truck and they draw their pistols and run forward. The co-driver of the truck is now lying in the bar ditch and when the truck clears his position the two men in the road are exposed directly in front of him and he opens fire on them with a pistol, dropping one of them dead in the road and wounding the other in the leg. The wounded man dives into the ditch on the other side of the road. The truck has come to a stop again, angled slightly toward the road, and the driver opens fire on the wounded man with a pistol from the truck window. The wounded man presses himself flat in the ditch and takes careful aim with his pistol and shoots the driver in the head. The driver's pistol clatters into the road. The co-driver in the ditch sees the pistol fall. He studies the far side of the road and then backs down into the ditch and crouches and runs along the ditch toward the truck. The wounded man sees the man's back moving along the ditch and he stands and fires three rounds after him. The last round hits the tank of the truck and brown sewage starts to spout from the hole. The co-driver reaches the truck and opens the door and clambers in over the body slumped in the floor and crouching over the body he reaches and pushes the clutch to the floor with his hand and drops the shifter into first gear and reaches and releases the emergency brake. He pushes down the accelerator with one hand and lets the clutch out with the other and the truck moves forward into the road. The wounded man climbs out of the ditch and hobbles back to the car and gets in and shuts the door. He lays the pistol on the seat and reaches under the seat and takes out an AR-15 machine-pistol and starts the car and pulls out down the road after the truck. The truck has wandered to the far side of the road and the car pulls up along the passenger side of the truck and the wounded man opens fire with the AR-15, emptying the magazine into the door of the truck. Then he slows the car and backs away and pulls to the verge and sits watching. The truck veers slowly off in front of him and rolls down into the bar ditch where it tilts up onto two wheels and balances for a moment and then drops back onto all four wheels and sits there in silence. The man in the car sits watching. In the rearview mirror he can see a car approaching, very small on the long stretch of blacktop road. He can see the pistol lying in the road and beyond that the dead body. He eases the car forward and comes abreast of the truck in the ditch and stops. He looks in the rearview mirror again. The approaching car is shimmering in the heatwaves off the road. The man's trouserleg is dark with blood to his boot. He places his hand on his thigh and leans forward slightly in pain. He turns the AR-15 on the seat and ejects the empty magazine and reaches under the seat and gets hold of a small canvas bag and puts it in his lap and unzips it and takes out a loaded magazine from among the half dozen in the bag and loads the AR-15 and pulls back the slide to chamber a round. The approaching car has slowed. Now it stops. It turns sideways in the road and backs up and swings around and heads back the way it came. The wounded man has opened the door and he steps out and levels the AR-15 and opens fire on the fleeing car. He empties the magazine and then lowers the gun and stands watching. The car slows and drifts off the road and down into the bar ditch and comes to a stop. The man reaches into the car and gets another magazine and reloads the AR-15 and turns and goes down the bank to the truck.

Sewage is still leaking from the bullethole in the tank. The man limps up to the passenger side of the truck with the gun at the ready and pulls open the door and steps back. Then he steps up and reaches into the truck and pulls out a body by the belt and lets it fall into the grass. Then he pulls the other one out on top of it. He turns and climbs up out of the ditch and stands in the road and looks up the road and down. He limps down the road to the car and gets the pistol and the pouch of magazines off the seat and takes the keys from the ignition and goes to the rear of the car and opens the trunk and gets out his bag. He opens the bag and puts in the machine-pistol and the magazines and closes it again. He puts the pistol in his belt at the small of his back and closes the trunk and walks down the road to the body and sets the bag in the road and takes his knife from his pocket and opens it and kneels painfully and cuts open the dead man's rear pocket and takes out the man's billfold and opens his bag and puts the billfold in and shuts the bag and gets to his feet and picks up the bag and goes back up the road toward the truck.

The man is sitting in the front seat of the septic-tank truck whittling with his knife on a treebranch. His open bag is sitting on the seat beside him. There is a box of nine-millimeter cartridges in the bag and he takes one of the cartridges out and compares the diameter of the bullet to the diameter of the stick he is whittling. Now he cuts a ring around the branch about three inches from the end.

The man climbs down from the cab of the truck and walks back and jams the end of the stick into the hole in the truck. He breaks off the branch and throws it to one side and folds away his knife and wipes his hands on his trousers and taps the plug in more firmly with the pistol and then goes back and climbs painfully up into the cab and shuts the door and rests for a minute with his eyes closed. Then he takes out his cell phone and dials a number and puts the phone to his ear.

WOUNDED MAN   Bueno. Tenemos la troca.

No. Más tiempo.

Por la mañana. Creo que sí.

Sí. A las siete, cómo no.

Problemas? No. Nada de importancia. Ándale pues.

He folds away the phone and rests for a few seconds. Then he starts the truck and drives up out of the ditch and the truck pulls away down the road, the gears shifting.

* * * * *

The woman with the red umbrella is walking up the street in the rain. A black Escalade pulls up alongside her splashing her with water from the gutter and two men get out. They come from behind with a cloth bag that has a leather belt around it and they pull this over her head and down almost to her knees and one of

*them pulls the strap and it draws shut instantly about her. They
then pick her up by the belt at either side and literally throw her
into the rear seat of the vehicle and shut the door and get in and
drive away leaving her purse and her poodle and her umbrella
on the sidewalk in the rain. Elapsed time about fifteen seconds.*

* * * * *

*The counselor is in the handicapped booth of the mens room at
an international airport talking on a cell phone.*

LAURA   I'm really worried, Baby.

COUNSELOR   It's going to be all right. I'll call you.

LAURA   Cant you meet me someplace?

COUNSELOR   I cant.

LAURA   That's not possible. That you cant.

COUNSELOR   God I miss you.

LAURA   Meet me.

COUNSELOR   We really have to be careful.

LAURA   You said that if they were looking for
               you they would have already found you.
               Isnt that what you said?

COUNSELOR   No. Not exactly.

LAURA   How bad is it? Baby?

Silence.

COUNSELOR   All right. Where.

LAURA   You say.

COUNSELOR   Alpha Centauri.

LAURA   That's too far. We'd be too old to do it. How about Boise?

COUNSELOR   Boise?

LAURA   Boise.

COUNSELOR   Why Boise?

LAURA   What's wrong with Boise?

COUNSELOR   Have you ever been to Boise?

LAURA   No. Have you?

COUNSELOR   No. What will you be wearing?

LAURA   A red dress.

COUNSELOR   What else?

LAURA   That's all.

COUNSELOR   No knickers.

LAURA   No.

COUNSELOR   Boise.

LAURA   Yes.

COUNSELOR   Do you have a hotel?

LAURA   I'm looking as we speak.

COUNSELOR   Wednesday.

LAURA   Tomorrow.

COUNSELOR   Wednesday. Leave me a message at the Delta Counter.

LAURA   I love you.

COUNSELOR   I love you.

The counselor folds the phone and drops it into the toilet and flushes it.

* * * * *

Plywood office of a junkyard in the desert. The junkyard man is talking on the phone. A pitbull lying on a mat at the side of his desk growls and stands up. The man looks up.

JUNKYARD MAN Tengo un cliente.

He hangs up the phone and looks at the client. The client comes forward in his bloodstained clothes and limps to a stop and reaches into his jacket. The junkyard man looks somewhat alarmed. The dog growls.

WOUNDED MAN Está bien. No le preocupe.

He takes a false-leather pouch with a bank logo from his coat and unzips it and takes out three banded sheafs of hundred-dollar bills and drops them onto the desk. The junkyard man stands up.

JUNKYARD MAN Cállete, Dulcinea. Cállete.

The dog lies down, grousing.

JUNKYARD MAN Siempre las más feroces, las perras.

The junkyard. The junkyard man is harrying two boys.

JUNKYARD MAN Ándale. Pronto! Pronto!

JUNKYARD BOY   Pero es un pickup.

JUNKYARD MAN Sí, sí. Claro. Es lo mismo. Sólo la
              frente es diferente. La cabina es
              la misma. La cabina y las puertas.
              Ándale.

*They run out through the lot, carrying a battered-looking
toolbox.*

*The septic-tank truck, parked in the junkyard lot. One of the
doors—bullet-riddled—is off and is standing against the front
wheel of the truck. A boy is unscrewing the other door with an
electric screwdriver while a second boy holds the door open. The
door is propped up on a crate with a two-by-four under its bottom edge and the second boy levers it up to take the weight off it.
It falls away and the two boys catch it and take it off and stand
it in the weeds against a wrecked car. The driver's door has exit
holes and the passenger door entry holes—and more of them.*

*The junkyard. The two boys with the toolbox catch the door
they've removed from a pickup truck and carry it down
past the rows of wrecked cars to the septic-tank truck.*

*The junkyard. The doorless septic-tank truck is being jacked
up on one side with two floor jacks. The junkyard man oper-
ates one of the jacks. The plug has been removed from the hole
in the tank and the sewage is leaking from the hole.*

JUNKYARD MAN Más atrás. Más.

The truck tilts up and the leak slows and then stops.

Junkyard. The owner is standing in a chair with welding goggles on and holding an oxyacetylene torch. He melts lead from a stick and spreads it over the bullethole in the tank with a wooden paddle.

Septic-tank truck. Two girls are scrubbing out the cab with brushes and pails of water. The seat is out of the truck. One of the doors has been put on and the junkyard man swings it shut and opens it again and adjusts the latch with a screwdriver. One of the boys is spray-painting the other door where it stands against some stacked parts with the window down.

A mobile home at the edge of the junkyard. A car pulls up in the drive and a woman gets out carrying a red plastic toolbox. She climbs the stairs where a girl holds the door for her.

Interior mobile home. The wounded man is lying on a cheap sofa with his leg stretched out on a coffeetable that is covered with a sheet. There is a plastic bucket in the floor with bloody gauze. The woman finishes wrapping his leg and turns and takes a syringe from her toolbox and unwraps it.

Reiner's house. Malkina's bedroom.

MALKINA   *(On the telephone)* Look. The last I heard they had just gone through Midland Texas. That was about twelve hours ago. Since then nothing. So I picked up the phone and called the sheriff and asked him if they had found any dead bodies along the highway down there and he said yes they had and I thanked him and hung up. I know you think I'm kidding. I'm not kidding. And I'm not out. And I'm not kidding about that either. And yes. I know where the truck is. All right. Really? Well I think that falls under the category of tough shit. We're all done here.

She hangs up the telephone.

* * * * *

City street at night. A light rain is falling. Reiner in the white Cadillac Escalade. The two cheetahs are in the rear. A black Escalade pulls past and turns in front of him and cuts him off and stops. Reiner hits the brakes and jams the gearshift into reverse and turns to back up, his arm over the back of the seat. The cheetahs are slammed about. Another Escalade pulls in behind him and he slams the shifter back into drive again and cuts the wheel to try to pull around the Escalade in front of him but it has backed up and he is trapped between the two vehicles. The driver has jumped out of the front Escalade and he comes to Reiner's window and slams a prybar against it but it only bounces off the glass. He slams it again. A second man comes up and waves him away and jams a device against the door that looks a bit like a shop router. He pulls down a lever over the top of the machine and it fires a plunger into

*the door with a sound like a pistol shot and he pushes another
lever up and pulls the door open with the device still attached.
He reaches in and grabs Reiner by the collar and pulls him
half way out of the vehicle. Reiner claws at his trouserleg and
comes up with a short barreled revolver from an ankle-holster.*

MAN WITH PRYBAR   Cuidado!

*The man pulling Reiner from his vehicle drops him and leaps
back and pulls an automatic pistol from the rear of his belt.
Reiner fires wildly and the man fires three rounds into Reiner
and Reiner slides out to lie face down in the street. His gun
clatters away. The man with the automatic pistol half turns
away and bangs the sides of his head with the heels of his fists
in frustration. The man with the prybar throws up his hands.*

MAN WITH PISTOL   Madre de Jesus! Hijo de puta!

*He kicks the dead man in the head and turns. He throws one
hand up in the air.*

MAN WITH PRYBAR   Vámanos.

*The man with the pistol shoves the gun into the back of his belt
and pulls up the lever on the doorjacker and pulls it away and
turns and kicks the corpse again.*

MAN WITH PISTOL   Pendejo.

*The two men turn and go back to the Escalade and get in and
pull away. The Escalade blocking Reiner's vehicle at the rear*

pulls past and follows and they disappear down the street in the rain. The two cheetahs at the rear window of the vehicle move to the side and sit looking out. A few people come forward from the surrounding buildings and stand looking. Two teenagers who are watching run out into the street and one takes Reiner's gun and the other his wristwatch and they take his billfold and turn him over face up and search the inside pockets of his coat and then they disappear in the rain. Reiner is lying face up in the street with the rain falling into his eyes.

* * * * *

City street in the rain. Night. Reiner is lying face up in the rain beneath the open door of the Escalade and the two cheetahs are crouched at either side of him and looking about furtively. One of them nudges Reiner's body with its nose.

* * * * *

Counselor on phone at his condominium.

COUNSELOR   I didnt think I'd reach you. Do you know where Reiner is?

WESTRAY   No.

COUNSELOR   He doesnt answer his cell and the phone at the club doesnt even ring.

WESTRAY   The club's closed. Some of Reiner's little friends showed up looking for

him and it wound up with them rough-
ing up some of the customers. All the
help ran out the back door. The cats
are gone. So that's pretty much that. I
mean if you wanted to get shot having
dinner you could just go to Juarez.

COUNSELOR   When was this?

WESTRAY   Two nights ago.

COUNSELOR   Have you talked to him?

WESTRAY   Yes.

COUNSELOR   What did he say?

WESTRAY   He said he was going to try and find
his cats. Before some dumb fucking
cop shot them—his words. They've got
these electronic tracking collars but
they can cover a hell of a lot of ground
in pretty short order. Where are you?

COUNSELOR   I'm home.

WESTRAY   I'm surprised you're still there.

COUNSELOR   I wont be in an hour.

WESTRAY   An hour.

COUNSELOR   Yeah.

WESTRAY   Well, you might want to think about whether you should loll around there all that long.

COUNSELOR   Where are you?

WESTRAY   I'm not at home.

Silence.

COUNSELOR   All right. I'm just going to throw some things in the car.

WESTRAY   In the car.

COUNSELOR   Yeah.

WESTRAY   What are you? A mental defective?

The counselor goes to the window and looks out.

COUNSELOR   What am I supposed to drive?

WESTRAY   I cant advise you, Counselor. Call a cab.

Silence.

WESTRAY   You're pretty quiet.

COUNSELOR   Yeah.

WESTRAY   Let me tell you something, Counselor.
            If your description of a friend is some-
            one who will die for you then you dont
            have any friends. All right. I've got
            to go.

COUNSELOR   All right.

WESTRAY   You take care now.

COUNSELOR   Yeah.

The phone clicks to dial tone.

* * * * *

*Back yard of a suburban middle class home. The two chee-
tahs are walking along the edge of the swimming pool. One
stops to sniff at the water. In the pool are two boys, aged eight
and ten. They stand frozen. A man reclining in a poolside
canvas chair lowers the paper he is reading to see what the
silence is about. He freezes, holding the paper at the level
of his chest. The cheetahs amble slowly along the edge of the
pool and out across the lawn. The man lowers the paper into
his lap. The two boys turn to look at him. The oldest turns
to look where the cheetahs have gone and turns to the man
again.*

BOY   Dad?

The man closes his eyes and raises one hand palm-out. Almost as if in blessing.

* * * * *

International Airport. Laura gets out of a rental car at the airport rental parking lot and pulls her bag over her shoulder and takes her suitcase off of the passenger seat and shuts the door.

Laura coming down the aisle of the parking lot trailing her suitcase on wheels behind her. A black Escalade is coming down the row behind her. At the end of the row of cars another Escalade pulls in front of her and stops. Two men get out. She turns but the other Escalade has pulled up behind her. She drops the handle of her suitcase and turns to run between the parked cars but a man seizes her by the arm and pushes her back toward the vehicle. She is struggling furiously but the other man grabs her hair and pulls her around and opens a switchblade knife in her face and she stops and lowers her head.

* * * * *

An upscale hotel room, king size bed, flowers in a vase on the dresser. Night. The counselor is at the window looking out at the rain.

Entrance to the hotel. The counselor is standing looking out at the street.

DOORMAN   Sir? Did you need a cab?

COUNSELOR   No. Thank you. I'm all right.

Hotel bar. The counselor is sitting at a small table in the corner. The waiter passes his table and stops.

WAITER   You all right here Sir?

COUNSELOR   Sorry?

WAITER   Can I bring you something?

COUNSELOR   No. Thank you.

The waiter turns to go and then turns back.

WAITER   Are you all right Sir?

The counselor looks up at the waiter.

COUNSELOR   Will you do something for me?

WAITER   Yessir. Of course.

The counselor takes out his billfold and takes out a card and hands it to the waiter.

COUNSELOR   That's my card. I'm a guest at the
             hotel. What I wish you would do for

me is go to the desk and see if I have any messages. I know you're wondering why I dont go myself. But I've bothered them so much I think they're beginning to figure me for some sort of nutcase and I'm afraid they'll stop looking.

WAITER   *(Taking the card)* You got it.

* * * * *

Hotel room. Boise, Idaho.

COUNSELOR   Baby, please answer. Please answer. I dont know where you are. And if I dont know where you are I dont know where I am. I dont. I was lost all my life. I cant be lost again. I cant, Baby. I cant. The world without you is nothing. Just nothing.

* * * * *

Law office. Juarez Mexico. The counselor and a Mexican attorney or abogado. He is seated at his desk, his crocodile boots crossed on the desk top. He looks thoughtful. The counselor sits waiting.

ABOGADO   *(Mexican accent)* All right. I will have to make a call. You understand. Then if it is all right it is all right. Dont put me in the center. Okay?

COUNSELOR   In the middle.

ABOGADO   In the middle. Yes.

COUNSELOR   What do I owe you.

ABOGADO   You owe me nothing, Counselor. We are friends. A handshake. Wait for me. Have a coffee. I will have a yes or a no.

The counselor rises and reaches across the desk. The abogado rises. They shake hands.

COUNSELOR   Thank you.

The counselor turns to go.

ABOGADO   Counselor.

COUNSELOR   *(Turning)* Yes.

ABOGADO   I will do what I can do. But you must know that this is the long shot.

COUNSELOR   Yes. I do. Thank you.

ABOGADO   You're not—what do you call it? In hiding?

COUNSELOR   No. I was hiding. Now I'm seeking.

ABOGADO   Of course.

COUNSELOR   Thank you.

The abogado nods.

*   *   *   *   *

The counselor on the phone in a hotel room in El Paso.

JEFE   *(Spanish accent)* Yes. But I can only tell you what I told our friend. That there is no one to talk to.

COUNSELOR   Could I come to the Florída?

JEFE   The Florída is closed.

COUNSELOR   I would do whatever you suggest.

JEFE   But I have nothing to suggest, Counselor.

COUNSELOR   We could meet someplace.

JEFE   We are meeting now.

COUNSELOR   There must be someone I could see.

JEFE	I am afraid that there is no longer such a person. That is a thing of the past. I am afraid that there is no one to see.
COUNSELOR	Please dont hang up.
JEFE	I have some time. It is all right. I am just having my lunch.
COUNSELOR	There are people there?
JEFE	There is no one here. The waiter. I enjoy to have my lunch alone. It is more peaceful.
COUNSELOR	I'm not sure that you understand my position.
JEFE	But I do, Counselor. I lost a son. Two years ago. I thought that someone would call. To demand money. But there was no call. I never saw my son again. He was sixteen.
COUNSELOR	I'm sorry.
JEFE	Where the bodies are buried in the desert is a certain world, Counselor. Where they are simply left in the street is another. That is a country hereto-

fore unknown to me. But it must have always been here, must it not?

COUNSELOR   I dont know.

JEFE   Sí, sí. Con hielo, por favor. I'm sorry. You were saying.

The counselor is clutching the phone and leaning with the heel of his hand against his forehead, his eyes closed. He opens his eyes.

COUNSELOR   I dont know what I was saying.

JEFE   People are waiting. For what? At some point you must acknowledge that this new world is at last the world itself. There is not some other world. It is not merely a he ate us.

COUNSELOR   Hiatus.

JEFE   I'm sorry.

COUNSELOR   Hiatus. I believe the word is hiatus.

JEFE   Hiatus. Thank you, Counselor.

Silence.

COUNSELOR   Will you help me?

JEFE	I would urge you to see the truth of your situation, Counselor. That is my advice. It is not for me to say what you should have done. Or not done. I only know that the world in which you seek to undo your mistakes is not the world in which they were made. You are at a cross in the road and here you think to choose. But here there is no choosing. There is only accepting. The choosing was done long ago.

Silence.

JEFE	Are you there, Counselor?
COUNSELOR	Yes.
JEFE	I dont mean to upset you, but reflective men often find themselves at a certain remove from the realities of life. In any case, to prepare a place in our lives for the tragedies to come is an economy few wish to practice. Do you know the works of Antonio Machado?
COUNSELOR	No. I know his name.
JEFE	A lovely poet. I think his work does not translate so well. But the spanish is very beautiful. He was a schoolteacher

and he married a very beautiful young girl whom he loved very much. And she died. And so he became a great poet.

COUNSELOR   I'm not going to become a great poet.

JEFE   Perhaps not. But even were you to do so, it would be of little help to you. Machado would have given every line he wrote for one more hour with his beloved. There is no rule of exchange here, you see. Grief transcends every value. A man would give whole nations to lift it from his heart. And yet with it you can buy nothing.

Silence. The counselor holds his wrist to his forehead, his eyes closed.

JEFE   When my son was lost to me I would not pray for that which I should most fervently have wished for. I could not.

COUNSELOR   A speedy death.

JEFE   I'm sorry.

COUNSELOR   Why are you telling me this?

JEFE   Because you stand at that crossing of which we spoke. You may dedicate your life to grief or not. The choice is yours. The assassin would claim you as well, but he will require your compliance. And of course he puts nothing of himself at hazard. He seeks to know what the warrior knows, but he has no stomach for the warrior's way. He is a usurper and a pimp. And as he is without courage he is greatly to be feared. He would explore that realm to which we are all consigned, but his way is to send an emissary. To bring his victim to the edge of the precipice with the greatest care and then lean to inquire if there be any news. Some word amid the sobbing. Amid the bleeding and the cries and the terror. Not even in the act of love will one be the object of such solicitude and such care.

COUNSELOR   Why are you telling me this?

JEFE   Because you cannot accept the reality of your life.

COUNSELOR   Why do you care?

JEFE   Do you love your wife so completely that you would take her place upon the wheel? Not die for her. That is easy.

But that your nerve would not fail you as they bend to buckle the straps?

COUNSELOR   Yes. Yes, damn you.

Silence.

JEFE   That is good to hear, Counselor.

COUNSELOR   What are you saying? Are you saying that this is possible?

JEFE   No. It is not possible. Sí. Un cafecito. Por favor. Negro. Negro, sí. Gracias. I'm sorry, Counselor.

COUNSELOR   You said I was that man. At that crossing.

JEFE   Yes. At the understanding that life will not take you back. I have no wish to paint the world in colors more somber than those it wears, but as the world gives way to darkness it becomes more and more difficult to dismiss the understanding that the world is in fact oneself. It is a thing which you have created, no more, no less. And when you cease to be so will the world. There will be other worlds. Of course. But they are the worlds of other men and your understanding of them was never more than an illusion anyway. Your world—the only one that matters—will be gone. And it will never come again. The extinction of all reality is a concept no resignation can encompass. Until annihilation comes. And all grand ideas are seen for what they are. And now I must go. I have calls to make, and then, if there is time, I will take a little nap.

The phone rings off.

* * * * *

Night. Malkina and the black weightlifter are driving through the outskirts of the city. She is sitting with a GPS and a tracking monitor for the transponder. A narrow two-lane blacktop road in the headlights. Some lights in the distance. They come to a crossroads and the weight-lifter slows and looks at her.

MALKINA   Left. Go left.

They drive slowly along the road. Suddenly one of the cheetahs crosses the road ahead of them in the lights.

MALKINA   *(Almost crying)* It's Silvia. Hi, Baby. Hi, Baby.

* * * * *

A garage, the septic-tank truck. There is a gantry crane over-head—a chain hoist that slides on iron rails—and a man in coveralls and welding glasses is slicing open the tank of the truck laterally from front to rear with a cutting torch.

Garage. A welder is on top of the tank welding a metal bar to the tank. There is a heavy metal hook bolted through the bar and a similar hook is already in place toward the front of the truck. He finishes and tips up his mask and stands and pulls the hoist toward him along the rails with its chains swinging.

Garage. The top half of the tank is being lifted by the two hooks and the chains from the single hook hanging from the pulley. Inside the severed tank lie four fifty-five gallon steel drums. The gantry crane moves down the rail and lowers the top of the tank to the concrete floor behind the truck and a worker—in coveralls and wearing a mask—unhooks the chains and then the gantry moves back over the truck and he hooks a crosschain to the first of the barrels and tightens it with its turnbuckle and the first of the drums is lifted out of the tank.

The washbay in the corner of the garage. The four drums are standing upright on pallets and the worker in coveralls and rubber boots is hosing them down with a steamwasher.

* * * * *

Streets of Juarez. There is a yellow police ribbon strung across sawhorses blocking off the street and in the middle distance is a car that has been machinegunned. One door is open and there is a dead body in the street. Police cars with their roof-lights strobing. In the foreground people are marching with signs and with banners. They contain large full color portraits of the missing. The signs say: Desaparecido, or Desaparecido with a date following. They say: Se Busca A with a name following. Some of the women carry umbrellas against the sun and some carry crosses of raw wood and crosses with wreaths mounted on them. A khaki-colored Army jeep with a soldier in battle-dress at the rear of a mounted machinegun fords its way through the crowd. The counselor is among the mourners, carrying a poster with a color photograph of Laura.

* * * * *

Three men in breathing masks at the washbay. One is in workclothes and one is in white coveralls. The third, well dressed in slacks and sportcoat, is the Buyer. The worker has an electric driver and is unfastening the tops of the drums. One of them is already open and the man in coveralls takes out four clear plastic bags each holding a kilo of cocaine. The worker unscrews the bolt on the second drum and lifts away the rim that circles the top of the drum and then lifts away the top of the drum and moves on to the next drum. The buyer follows the man in coveralls across the garage. They have removed their masks.

BUYER   Why are there four drums?

COVERALL MAN   *(Mexican accent)* I dont know. I think
                   maybe we have a traveler.

BUYER	A traveler?
COVERALL MAN	Yes. A free rider. How do you say? Like you have on a ship. A something away.
BUYER	A stowaway?
COVERALL MAN	Yes. A stowaway.
WORKMAN	Madre de Jesus!

The coverall man turns, smiling. The workman has left the washbay and he has pulled away his mask and is almost gagging.

WORKMAN	Son of a beetch!
COVERALL MAN	Cierrelo! Pronto! Pronto!

He turns and goes through a metal door, laughing. The Buyer follows him up a set of concrete steps, iron pipe railing.

A small office with a glass window looking down to where the septic-tank truck is parked. Coverall man and the Buyer are sitting at a cheap metal table. There are computers on the table. A scale and some plates and the plastic bags of cocaine.

BUYER	In the last two accounts we're only an hour different. But it's another day. It's tomorrow.

COVERALL MAN	Yes. I love that.
BUYER	We're okay. We have what? Four hours?
COVERALL MAN	Yes. Perhaps we should know if electronic money earns an extra day of interest when it crosses the International Date Line.
BUYER	Good question. Why do they send you a dead body?
COVERALL MAN	No reason. It is convenient.
BUYER	Convenient.
COVERALL MAN	Yes. There is always somebody you wish for him to go away. So you send him to America.
BUYER	Do you know who he is?
COVERALL MAN	No. Of course not. He is a pasajero.
BUYER	A passenger?
COVERALL MAN	Yes. An immigrant.
BUYER	It's just a way to get rid of a body.

COVERALL MAN   Yes. Just a way. Somebody you dont
                    want around.

BUYER   From Mexico.

COVERALL MAN   From Colombia.

BUYER   He came from Colombia.

COVERALL MAN   Yes. Of course.

BUYER   What will you do with him?

COVERALL MAN   Nothing. He goes back in the truck.

BUYER   He goes back in the truck.

COVERALL MAN   Of course.

BUYER   And then what?

COVERALL MAN   Nothing. It is normal. Well. Not so
                    normal I suppose. They think it is
                    funny. A sort of joke. You have to
                    have a sense of humor in this busi-
                    ness.

BUYER   So what happens to him?

COVERALL MAN   Nothing. The truck goes back to-
                    gether. They paint it. He is inside.

He rides around. Maybe they sell the truck. At auction maybe. It's all the same. He rides around some more. Sucking up the shit. Welcome to America.

He smiles broadly. He checks the time by his Rolex.

* * * * *

A cafe in a border town. The counselor is lying at one of the cheap formica tables with his head in his folded arms, the photograph poster of Laura on the table.

CAFE MAN   Señor.

COUNSELOR   Yes.

CAFE MAN   Señor.

The counselor sits up and looks at the man.

CAFE MAN   I must close.

COUNSELOR   I know.

The counselor is haggard and unshaven.

CAFE MAN   What you do? You have no place to go maybe.

COUNSELOR   You dont have to go home but you cant stay here.

CAFE MAN   Cómo?

COUNSELOR   It's all right.

The counselor rises, picking up the photograph.

COUNSELOR   I fell asleep. I'm sorry.

CAFE MAN   There is no harm.

COUNSELOR   No harm. Lovely thought. Magical thought.

CAFE MAN   Cómo?

COUNSELOR   Good night.

CAFE MAN   Es muy peligroso. En las calles.

COUNSELOR   I know.

CAFE MAN   They hear somebody in the street they shoot them. Then they turn on the light to see who is dead.

COUNSELOR   Why do they do that?

CAFE MAN	*(Shrugging)* To make a joke. To show that death does not care. That death has no meaning.
COUNSELOR	Qué piensa? Usted. Do you believe that?
CAFE MAN	No. Of course not. All my family is dead. I am the one who has no meaning.
COUNSELOR	Entiendo.
CAFE MAN	Cuidado. Sí?
COUNSELOR	Sí. Cuidado.
CAFE MAN	Quién es? La Señora.
COUNSELOR	*(Turning at the door)* Mi esposa.
CAFE MAN	Ah. Guapa. Lo siento.

The counselor stands at the door.

COUNSELOR	Sí. Guapa. What is that?
CAFE MAN	It means she is beautiful.
COUNSELOR	No. I mean what does that mean? What is it? Beautiful.

CAFE MAN   I dont know. It is late.

COUNSELOR   Yes. Good night.

CAFE MAN   Good night, Amigo. Good night.

*   *   *   *   *

The counselor goes down an alley to a door and takes out a key and lets himself in. A bleak hallway, linoleum floor. A lightbulb hanging from the ceiling. He lets himself in at the first door on the right and turns on the light. A room with an iron bed and a cheap dresser and a sink. He fastens the chain and crosses to the bed and sits. He puts his poster on the bed beside him and lowers his face into his hands. Machinegun fire briefly in the distance.

*   *   *   *   *

International Airport. Westray exits carrying a medium-sized bag and a shoulder bag. He is dressed in a dark suit. He stands at the curb studying the cabs and limousines and then he crosses the street to a black town car and opens the door and gets in. The driver is an attractive woman who wears a chauffeur's cap. She turns and smiles at him.

WESTRAY   Me gusta su sombrero.

CHAUFFEUR   Thank you.

WESTRAY	The International.
CHAUFFEUR	*(Smiling)* I know.

She turns and starts the engine and they pull out into the traffic.

*   *   *   *   *

Desk at a major hotel in a world city. Westray is standing at the counter with his passport and credit card. He is waiting while the clerk checks his reservation. A very attractive blonde is standing a few feet away, checking in. She is dressed in a dark business suit and carries a large shoulder bag. Westray looks her over. She glances at him.

WESTRAY	How are you doing?
BLONDE	Okay. You're Canadian.
WESTRAY	You saw my passport. Where are you from?
BLONDE	New Mexico.
WESTRAY	Have a drink with me.
BLONDE	What?
WESTRAY	Have a drink with me. You're not married.

BLONDE   No.

WESTRAY   Get checked in. We can sit right over
                there. They'll bring us whatever we
                want.

BLONDE   You're a masher.

WESTRAY   A masher? Lord. Where did you hear
                that?

BLONDE   I'm teasing. I think.

WESTRAY   I'm a very decent chap. You'll see.

BLONDE   Do you have any references?

WESTRAY   Mmm. This is getting better all the
                time.

                        *   *   *   *   *

*World city. Malkina, dressed in a business suit, is crossing the
street. She walks down the sidewalk to a jeweler's window and
stands looking at the display behind the glass.*

*Sidewalk cafe in the city. Malkina is looking at a scrap of
paper and talking to the blonde from the hotel desk.*

MALKINA   Five digits. Who's Rowena?

BLONDE	I dont know.
MALKINA	Social. His driver's license is Nevada?
BLONDE	Yes.
MALKINA	All right. Your little bonus is in an envelope in my purse.

The Blonde opens one of two purses on the table and takes out the envelope and puts it in the other purse.

BLONDE	You still wont have his computer.
MALKINA	I'll have the computer. Were you planning on seeing him again?
BLONDE	What would be the point? He'll be broke.
MALKINA	Smart girl.
BLONDE	Or is it worse than that?
MALKINA	What do you care?
BLONDE	I dont want to get mixed up in something heavy.
MALKINA	You already are.

BLONDE	How do you mean?
MALKINA	What if he were to come looking for you?
BLONDE	But he wont. Will he?
MALKINA	No. He wont.

The Blonde sits staring at the sidewalk.

| BLONDE | Oh, Jesus. |

She gets up and takes her purse and takes out the envelope and puts it on the table.

MALKINA	What's that?
BLONDE	I dont want it.
MALKINA	Dont be a sap.
BLONDE	I cant. I have to go.
MALKINA	Well. Please yourself. You know what I like about Americans?
BLONDE	*(Blinking back the tears, angry)* No. What?
MALKINA	*(Smiling)* You can depend on them.

* * * * *

Morning. The counselor is asleep on the cot with his clothes on. There is a knocking at the door. He sits up. The knocking again.

COUNSELOR   Momento. Momento.

He crosses the room and undoes the chain and opens the door. A young man is standing there holding a package.

DELIVERY BOY   Está el abogado?

COUNSELOR   Sí.

The boy hands him the package and smiles and touches his cap and turns to go.

COUNSELOR   Momento. Qué es este?

The boy is at the outer door. He turns and holds out both hands.

DELIVERY BOY   Yo no sé. Un regalo. Quién sabe? Ábralo.

The boy goes out. The counselor goes back into his room and sits on the cot looking at the package. It is about five inches square and wrapped in paper and tied with a blue ribbon. He pulls the ribbon loose and it falls to the floor. He unwraps the paper and sits looking at a DVD. Suddenly he realizes what it is and he turns and drops it onto the bed like something hot and clutches at his face, his hands clawed.

COUNSELOR   Oh God. Oh God. Oh God.

* * * * *

A major street, world city. Westray comes out of a large build-
ing, possibly a bank. He is dressed in a tan summer business
suit and he is carrying a small black canvas bag. As he exits
into the street a man comes up behind him and drops the wire
of a bolito over his head and pulls the wire taut by its loop.
Westray instantly drops the bag and seizes the wire about his
neck and turns, wild-eyed. The assassin picks up the bag in
one movement and steps from the curb into the street where he
gets into a taxicab that is waiting for him with the door open.
The cab pulls away into the traffic.

Westray turning, the fingers of one hand caught in the wire
now being severed and the wire drawing into his neck. His
collar is red with blood. He sits down on the pavement and
kicks his feet, as if in annoyance. Almost like a petulant child.
Pedestrians have begun to stop, although at a distance. The
gearmotor of the bolito is grinding. Westray falls over, kick-
ing. His left carotid artery bursts and bright red blood sprays
in a fountain into the air and splashes back on the sidewalk.
The spectators draw back.

Inside the cab Malkina is sitting in the back seat with the
assassin. She takes the case and puts it in her lap and unzips
it and sorts through it. She takes out a computer and she looks
through the papers in a folder. She unzips a pocket in the case
and takes out a pair of passports. She takes out an envelope. A
jump drive. She puts all these things in her shoulder bag and
takes out an envelope and hands it to the assassin and he puts

it in his shirt and she zips shut her shoulder bag and leans and
taps the cabdriver on the shoulder.

MALKINA   Aquí, por favor.

CABDRIVER   Aquí?

MALKINA   Sí.

The cab pulls to the curb and Malkina hands the driver some
bills and gets out and shuts the door. The cabdriver looks at
the money and purses his mouth in surprise and approval. He
turns to the man in the back.

CABDRIVER   A dónde?

The assassin is watching Malkina as she disappears among the
pedestrians. Her elegant fitted clothes.

*   *   *   *   *

Sidewalk cafe. World city. Malkina at a table with Lee—a
twenty-five-year-old Chinese American.

LEE   What do you have? Do you have the
               CAs?

MALKINA   I have two of them.

LEE   Can you get the other two?

MALKINA   Yes. I've got a search engine download-
             ing them out of another computer.

LEE   There's another player.

MALKINA   No. He's out of the picture.

LEE   How far out?

MALKINA   All the way out.

LEE   You're sure.

MALKINA   Very sure.

Lee studies her.

LEE   Do you ever get a sudden dark feeling
             about something?

MALKINA   Concerning a deal?

LEE   Concerning anything.

MALKINA   I dont know. But I could imagine that
             my dark and your dark are different
             darks.

LEE   All right.

MALKINA	I'll have everything by tomorrow that there is to get. What we dont have we'll just have to figure out. I've got the routing numbers and the account numbers. I've got the source code but we'll have to have a compiler to translate everything into machine-readable code. It's all doable.
LEE	VPNs and routers.
MALKINA	Yes.
LEE	Passwords.
MALKINA	What is it you really want to know?
LEE	There's somebody else. Your bank guy?
MALKINA	He gets ten percent and all his costs come out of his end.
LEE	Are you Ukrainian?
MALKINA	No. Soy pura Porteña.
LEE	All right.
MALKINA	You dont have to worry about my connections. I'm an independent operator.

LEE	I worry about everything. That's why I'm still in business. This is basically a spoof.
MALKINA	If you like.
LEE	All right. What is it that *you* want to know?
MALKINA	I'd like to know how clean you are.
LEE	I dont keep anything around that I dont have to.
MALKINA	Yes. Well you can have a basic tool kit with Sequel servers and whatever but a remote access Trojan Horse like Zrizbi or Torig is not for keeping track of your household expenses.
LEE	It's not illegal to own one.
MALKINA	That's not the point. When they find it they keep looking.
LEE	Okay.
MALKINA	You can clone your cell phone with a SIM writer but the bills keep going to the number you're cloned off of so you cant use it forever.

LEE   We dont want to use it forever.

MALKINA   I know. But you dont know how much
             time you have. Forever can be pretty
             fucking short. Plus hackers think you
             cant trace a cloned cell phone but that's
             not really true any more. And if they get
             a trace they can use a Stingray and locate
             you physically to within about five feet.
             You dont want that in your life.

LEE   All right. How many calls total, four?

MALKINA   Yes.

LEE   Voice crypt.

MALKINA   Yes. Separate shoes.

LEE   Yeah, well, on the subject of security I
             know that you understand nothing gets
             off the hard drive, but this would still
             come under the heading of time con-
             straints.

MALKINA   I'm not worried about that. What's out
             there is out there. They think their
             traffic analysis is sophisticated but by
             definition it has to lag the protocols
             that generate it. As for the physical
             computers you just put them in the

oven and set it to four-fifty and walk away. Everything I need to take with me I can download onto a USB stick.

LEE   Double encrypted.

MALKINA   Yes.

LEE   Random seed.

MALKINA   Yes.

LEE   All right. Let me look at it. We havent talked money.

MALKINA   Quarter mil.

LEE   I dont suppose you'd tell me what the caper is worth.

MALKINA   Why not? You're going to see it up on the screen anyway. It's twenty-two mill, give or take whatever. And if we nail all four accounts.

LEE   You could boot that quarter up a bit.

MALKINA   All right.

LEE   Five hundred K.

MALKINA   That's not a bit. That's double.

LEE   Four hundred.

MALKINA   Done.

LEE   Cash.

MALKINA   Cash. Do you need something up front?

LEE   No. I'm good. What are you going to do, float a bank loan?

MALKINA   Something like that.

* * * * *

City street. Ambulance siren. The ambulance pulls up onto the sidewalk where Westray is lying, parting the crowd. Three medics get out and go to the body and place a sheet over it and one of them takes a pulse at the wrist and then they get a gurney out of the ambulance and place it on the sidewalk and one of the medics picks up the body by the feet and the other two take hold at either side and they lift the body onto the gurney still covered by the sheet. A gasp goes up from the crowd and when the medics turn to look Westray's severed head is still lying on the sidewalk together with the bolito.

* * * * *

Landfill on the outskirts of Juarez. Bleak desert landscape with raw mountains hazy in the distance. Sound of a bull- dozer. The landfill is a rubble of nameless trash. There are fires burning and smoke drifts across the fill. Families in the distance are picking through the garbage. Women and chil- dren. They carry woven shopping bags over their shoulders. A few buzzards strut about. An old ten-ton dumptruck labors across the landfill and turns and halts and backs and comes to a stop and the driver pulls the lever and the bed tips up and dumps its load of trash. The driver jiggles the lever and the bed clangs and then he lowers the bed into place and the truck lumbers away. A dusty yellow bulldozer pulls up and begins to grade the trash away into the fill. A girl's body comes up in the trash and then rolls under again. The bulldozer backs and then goes forward again. The headless body of Laura in her red dress appears briefly and then disappears in the trash and garbage.

* * * * *

World city, apartment in a high rise building. Night. The reflection of Lee's face in the glass. Reflection of a bank of computers behind him. The lights of the city below. Malkina crosses the room and then crosses back.

Lee and Malkina sitting at the computers. She is wearing a set of headphones. Lines of text running on the screens.

LEE   What's the time delay again?

MALKINA   *(Taking off headset)* What?

LEE   I'm just rattling your cage.

MALKINA   Dont.

LEE   All right.

Malkina brings tea from the kitchen. They sit at the screens.

MALKINA   We've got two hours.

LEE   You want to try and get some sleep? I'll
                 wake you.

MALKINA   I'm too wired.

LEE   You want to go for a walk?

MALKINA   I'm not leaving this suite if the build-
                 ing catches fire. You can see what's on
                 television if you like.

LEE   What if it's us?

MALKINA   I dont know. Maybe they have virtual
                 prisons for virtual felons.

*   *   *   *   *

Arizona high plains. The male cheetah is lying under a tree. He gets up and walks out to the edge of the grass and stands looking into the distance.

* * * * *

A penthouse restaurant in a major city at night, the lights of the city spread out below. Malkina is at the door being greeted by the maitre d'.

MAITRE D'   Buena noches, Señora. Buena noches.

With her is a tall and elegant man in his forties dressed in a black business suit with an expensive gold silk tie. The maitre d' holds out his hand for them to enter.

MAITRE D'   Bienvenidos. Bienvenidos.

She is dressed in an ankle-length black pleated skirt, a dark green bolero jacket with black braiding. She wears a heavy graduated swag choke necklace of emeralds with matching earrings. She is about five months pregnant, just noticeable. They cross through the room and the maitre d' gestures them to a window table where a waiter holds a chair for her. A second waiter is unfolding their napkins and a third is crossing the room with a champagne bucket on a pedestal which he positions at the man's elbow. He lifts a bottle of Dom Pérignon from the bucket and wraps it with a towel and twists out the cork and pours two flutes of the champagne and then twists the bottle back into the ice. The maitre d' bows.

MAITRE D'   Buen appetivo.

He moves away. They touch glasses. The escort speaks with an accent possibly European.

ESCORT   To the heir then.

MALKINA   Thank you.

ESCORT   Will you return to the States then? At that time?

MALKINA   I dont think so.

ESCORT   Where will you go?

MALKINA   I can go wherever I choose.

ESCORT   To Europe?

MALKINA   There's not going to be a Europe. I think I might like China.

ESCORT   China. Really?

MALKINA   Yes.

ESCORT   You dont speak the language.

MALKINA   *(Smiling)* I'm a quick study.

ESCORT   How do you get money into China?

MALKINA   It's not a problem. You can buy into
              the market. Heavy industries are good.
              Pohang Iron and Steel I like.

ESCORT   What about cash?

MALKINA   The easiest way to compress wealth is
              with diamonds. They're highly negotia-
              ble and they weigh nothing. Although a
              Picasso painting—out of the frame and
              rolled up—is worth about the same.
              Ounce for ounce.

ESCORT   And how much would that be?

MALKINA   *(Smiling)* Is this an idle curiosity?

ESCORT   It's a curiosity.

MALKINA   There are roughly a hundred and fifty
              carats in an ounce. And diamonds aver-
              age out to about ten thousand dollars
              a carat. Stones in the two to five carat
              range. Can you do the math?

ESCORT   You do it.

MALKINA   Diamonds are worth about one point
              five million an ounce. You can hold

twenty million dollars in the palm of your hand. Money itself weighs out at about three thousand dollars to the ounce. Roughly fifty thousand dollars a pound. So that twenty mil in your hand would be over four hundred pounds of paper in hundred-dollar bills. Four forty, to be exact.

ESCORT   Can you sell diamonds in China?

MALKINA   You can sell diamonds on Mars.

ESCORT   What if it's a girl? Wouldnt that be a problem?

MALKINA   It would. But he's not.

ESCORT   I see. May I ask you something?

MALKINA   You may ask.

ESCORT   Is the child Reiner's?

MALKINA   Is that what you want to know?

ESCORT   Yes.

MALKINA   No. It's not. Reiner had had a vasectomy. The counselor used to tell people that it was court-ordered. I told him the day that I found out. He was all right with it. He wanted me to get an abortion and we would go on as if nothing had happened. He was actually somewhat emotional about it. It surprised me. I told him that if it was a girl I would abort it. But it wasnt. And I didnt.

ESCORT   Did he want to know whose it was?

MALKINA   Of course.

ESCORT   Did you tell him?

MALKINA   No.

ESCORT   The child will have no father.

MALKINA   Every child has a father. In this case the best kind of father.

ESCORT   And what kind of father is that?

MALKINA   The best kind of father is a dead father.

ESCORT   You are serious.

MALKINA   I think that Freud is right in that a son who is worshipped by his mother will never doubt himself. But a contentious father can undo that. And the virtues of a dead father—his very identity for that matter—are limited only by the mother's imagination. You look a bit uncomfortable.

ESCORT   I'm fine.

MALKINA   If I were a woman that you could have, then you would not be interested. The curse of the player.

ESCORT   I hope that is not true.

MALKINA   *(Smiling)* No one wants to admit that the object of his desire has weighed him in the balance and found him wanting. That is a very hard thing to accept. Better to imagine the desired one as whimsical and irresolute. Would you agree?

ESCORT   *(Smiling)* You are quite cruel.

MALKINA   You will thank me.

ESCORT   What is it that *you* want?

MALKINA   My own life. I own very little. Some jewelry. A few clothes. There are times when I imagine that I would like my innocence back. If I ever had it. But I would never pay the price which it now commands on the market.

ESCORT   *(Nodding. Looking up at her. Quietly)* Your own life.

MALKINA   *(Studying him. Then)* When the world itself is the source of your torment then you are free to exact vengeance upon any least part of it. I think perhaps you would have to be a woman to understand that. And you will never know the depth of your hurt until you are presented with the opportunity for revenge. Only then will you know what you are capable of.

ESCORT   I think you have told me more than I wished to know.

MALKINA   It's all right.

ESCORT   And the cats?

MALKINA   Silvia died. She had a congenital heart condition. Which we knew. Raoul is alive and well in Arizona. He rules over a domain of a thousand hectares and he has a special rock where he can take the sun and watch for game. That's all. Dogs bring people together. Cats dont. Still, I miss him.

ESCORT   Raoul.

MALKINA   *(Smiling)* Yes. Raoul. I miss watching him bring down jackrabbits out on the desert at seventy miles an hour. I never tired of that. To see quarry killed with elegance is very moving to me. It always was.

ESCORT   Is it sexual?

MALKINA   Of course. A thing like that is always sexual. But grace. Freedom. The hunter has a purity of heart that exists nowhere else. I think he is not defined so much by what he has come to be as by all that he has escaped being. You can make no distinction between what he is and what he does. And what he does is kill. We of course are another matter. I suspect that we are ill-formed for the path we have chosen. Ill-formed and ill-prepared. We would like to draw a veil over all that blood and terror. That have brought us to this place. It is our faintness of heart that would close our eyes to all of that, but in so doing it makes of it our destiny. Perhaps you would not agree. I dont know. But nothing is crueler than a coward, and the slaughter to come is probably beyond our imagining. Should we think about ordering? I'm famished.

CREDITS

picador.com

blog
videos
interviews
extracts